I AM CANADA

DEADLY VOYAGE

RMS *Titanic*

by Hugh Brewster

Scholastic Canada Ltd.

Toronto New York London Auckland Sydney
Mexico City New Delhi Hong Kong Buenos Aires

Copyright © 2011 by Hugh Brewster. All rights reserved.

A Dear Canada Book. Published by Scholastic Canada Ltd.
SCHOLASTIC and I AM CANADA and logos are trademarks
and/or registered trademarks of Scholastic Inc.

Library and Archives Canada Cataloguing in Publication

Brewster, Hugh
Deadly voyage : RMS Titanic / Hugh Brewster.

(I am Canada)
ISBN 978-1-4431-0465-4

1. Titanic (Steamship)--Juvenile fiction. I. Title.
II. Series: I am Canada

PS8603.R49D43 2011   jC813'.6   C2011-902617-1

6 5 4 3 2 1   Printed in Canada 114   11 12 13 14 15

The display type was set in Decotura.
The text was set in Minion.

First printing September 2011

To my mother

PROLOGUE

*The last survivor. That's what the young man
on the phone called me. He claimed that I'm the
last Canadian still alive from the Titanic. I was
surprised to hear this, since there were quite a few of
us on board. Then he invited me to a convention for
people interested in the Titanic. And that surprised
me even more — I thought the Titanic would
be long forgotten by now! I said I was too old to
travel, so he asked me to write down my memories
of the ship and what happened the night she sank.
He said that there are too many myths about the
Titanic, and I had to agree with him on that. The
newspapers back then had a field day making up
wild stories about it. And many of those outrageous
things are still believed today. But the real story is
quite amazing enough. I know because I was there.
I saw it happen. It's time to set the record straight.*

— James Laidlaw, April 15, 1987

CHAPTER ONE
THE BOAT TRAIN

Waterloo Station, London, April 10, 1912, 9:30 a.m.

"Jamie, *do* hurry on," my father called out over the noise in the station. He was standing beside a porter and a luggage-filled trolley. "We *know* what the platform is," he added impatiently as I stared up at the signboard.

"It's Platform 12," I announced.

"Yes, the porter *knows* that," he sighed. "It's his job."

Boat Train–Southampton had been posted in white letters on the signboard below a list of places that all seemed to start with *W* — Wimbledon, Wandsworth, Winchester and Woking. But I especially liked the name Boat Train. It made me think of a large boat that went barrelling along the railway tracks. Of course, I knew that it was just a train that *took* you to the boat. But in this case the train at Waterloo Station wasn't taking us to just *any* boat. It was taking us to the largest boat in the world. My father had given me a brochure

3

about the *Titanic* and I couldn't wait to explore this giant, brand new ship. It had a swimming pool and a gymnasium and dining rooms where I could order anything I wanted. After the terrible food at my English boarding school, I was ready to eat until I burst.

We actually needed two porters to wheel all our luggage to Platform 12. My mother had spent weeks supervising the packing up of our rented house in Kent. Crates of furniture and most of our belongings had already been sent back to Canada on another ship. But we still had a mountain of luggage going with us on the *Titanic*. My mother had decided she had to have a different gown to wear for dinner each night on board the ship — why, I'll never know.

Rosalie, my mother's maid, was walking with Maxwell, our Airedale terrier, beside the second luggage trolley. I went back and took his leash. "Come on Maxwell, come on boy, we're going on a big, big boat!" I said. I asked Rosalie in French if she was happy to be going home to Montreal — even though I already knew the answer.

"So, so much," she answered in English as we followed my parents through the crowded station.

At Platform 12, I spotted the shiny dark-brown coaches of the waiting Boat Train. The porters unloaded the trunks into the luggage car and then pushed the trolleys with the smaller bags along the platform until they found an empty compartment for us. I gave Maxwell's leash back to Rosalie and started to lift one of the bags from a trolley, but the porters waved me off, saying, "We'll do it, son. We'll do it."

Wisps of steam floated around the wheels of the green locomotive at the front of the train. I noticed that the conductor was standing with his whistle in his mouth — clearly we didn't have much time! The porters hurriedly placed our hand luggage into the overhead racks as we sank into the seats underneath them. My father paid the porters, who tipped their hats and hopped back onto the platform. The moment the conductor's whistle blew, doors slammed and the locomotive built up steam. I looked at my watch, which read 9:45 a.m. The compartment gave a sudden jolt — we were off!

Maxwell started to bark, so I patted his head to calm him. As we left the station, the train went into a tunnel, and when it emerged I could see the sooty back walls of London tenement buildings. On their slate roofs stood tall chimneys with smoke coming out of red clay chimney pots. Sometimes when a heavy fog rolled into London it would cause a "pea souper," a smog so dense it would blank out the sun and make morning seem like dusk. But today a fresh April breeze had blown the smoke away and there was an occasional burst of sunshine through the clouds

Soon we reached the London suburbs, with tulips and fruit trees blooming in neatly tended gardens. Finally we reached open country, where stone churches with square towers stood beside green fields lined with hedgerows that were just coming into leaf. I saw a horse clip-clopping along a laneway, hauling a cart filled with tin milk cans.

"So-o lovely," my mother said with a sigh. "I shall really miss the English countryside, won't you, Henry?"

My father looked up briefly from his newspaper and mumbled agreement.

"I won't miss the rain," I said, "that's for sure."

"Or the damp," added Rosalie.

"Montreal is very cold in the winter, you mustn't forget that," my mother replied.

I felt like saying that I'd never been as cold in Canada as I had been in my freezing boarding house at school. But I could see that my mother was sad to be leaving England, so I kept silent. We soon passed through a place called Basingstoke and not long after that, a town with a huge grey cathedral right in the centre of it came into view. Suddenly I knew where we were.

"That's Winchester!" I called out. "We'll be going right by the school!"

"So we shall," my father said, looking up from his newspaper.

When we first arrived in England, he had decided that I should go to Winchester College because the son of a man he worked with at the Imperial Bank had gone there.

"It's the oldest school in England," he had said. "And you'll learn how to play cricket. But you'll have to pass the entrance exam first."

I did well on the admission test, though I never quite got the hang of cricket. But the school certainly was old — older than anything in Canada, as I was frequently reminded — founded in 1382, over a hundred years before Columbus sailed the ocean blue. A few of the school buildings dated back to that time and had Latin inscriptions on them. Latin was a big deal at Winchester. We had to say prayers in chapel in Latin and also the grace before meals. Even the school song was sung in that dead language — never my favourite subject.

But much worse than any Latin class were the prefects — older boys who were allowed to boss around younger boys like me. In my first year I had had to polish shoes and do other chores for one prefect — a fat, pompous fellow with a wobbly chin, named Sykes. I can still hear him bellowing *"Coll-ie-e!"* at the top of his lungs, meaning that I had to scurry and see what he wanted me to do. Collie was his oh-so-clever nickname for me, short for Colonial Boy. It didn't help that my hair tended to poke up around my ears like a collie dog, so the nickname just stuck.

The train slowed enough as we passed through Winchester that I caught a glimpse of the school's cricket pitch and rugby fields. I thought of the droning voice of the headmaster at morning prayers. I thought of the icy cold-water baths we had to take. And I could almost smell the dining hall, where the odour of boiled cabbage or soggy Brussels sprouts always lingered. It was thought to be a big treat when we had smoked fish called kippers for breakfast. And a frequent dessert — or sweet, as the English called it — was gluey tapioca with a dollop of strawberry jam in it. The boys called it "nosebleed pudding."

"I am so-o happy to be out of that prison," I whispered to Rosalie. She giggled and my father looked up from his paper disapprovingly.

About half an hour later we entered the outskirts of a larger town, which I guessed must be

Southampton. I reached up and pulled my bag down from the overhead rack.

"Plenty of time yet, my lad," said my father.

When I put my head against the window and looked forward, I could see in the distance what looked like large cranes towering over the buildings ahead of us. They must be used for loading freight at the Southampton docks, I thought. As we drew closer I caught a glimpse of the funnels and masts of some ships, but none of them looked big enough to be the *Titanic*. We then crossed over a main roadway and went right onto the pier under the overhanging roof of a long train shed. As we slowed to a stop I walked into the corridor beside our compartment and looked out the window. Maxwell followed me and put his paws up on the window.

All we could see through the glass was an enormous wall of black steel with about a million rivets in it, and higher up, a row of round portholes. Then I realized that the train had pulled in right next to the giant black hull of the *Titanic*.

"Let's find a porter, Jamie," my father called as doors opened on the other side of the train. I led Maxwell back to our compartment, hoisted my brown leather school bag onto my shoulders and stepped out onto the platform. My father had already hailed two red-uniformed porters. As they were loading our luggage onto their trolleys, Maxwell began to paw at my leg.

"Maxwell needs to do his business," I said to my father.

"That's a bit of a nuisance," he replied.

I told him not to worry and that I'd take care of Max while they went on ahead.

"Very well, but don't be long," he said. "We'll meet you on the other side of the gangway. You just climb those stairs where the other passengers are going."

"Don't you think we should wait here for him?" my mother asked.

"The boy's fourteen, Margaret," my father replied. "He'll be fine."

Maxwell was starting to yelp so I ran off with him down the platform to the end of the train. We both jumped down onto the tracks and he instantly squatted to relieve himself. As I looked across, the *Titanic* seemed even bigger than she had from inside the train. The *Empress of Britain*, the ship we had taken across the Atlantic two years ago, would look like a tugboat next to her.

The sun broke through the clouds, making the ship's white-painted upper decks gleam in the sunshine. I looked left to see if I could make out the name *TITANIC* on her bow, but it was too far away. By craning my neck backwards, though, I could just see the ship's four giant funnels pointing upward to the clouds.

When Maxwell was finished we jumped back onto the platform and headed for the stairs. On the second level was a long verandah that hung out over the train, and an awning that covered the entrance to a gangway that went across to the ship. By now most of the train passengers had gone on board, but in the middle of the gangway was a man taking a photograph. From where he stood, the side of the *Titanic* looked like a giant cliff face.

"That'll make a great picture," I said as I approached him, wishing I had a camera with me.

He clicked the shutter and turned to me with a smile. "She's far too big to do in one shot," he said in an Irish accent.

I nodded and walked past him into the vestibule. My parents were standing farther inside, near the curved banister of a massive staircase.

"Here he is," my mother said to the green-jacketed steward who was waiting with them. She had a small bunch of flowers in her hand and my father was sporting a red carnation on his jacket. I was given one too so I stuck it into the buttonhole of my school blazer.

I started to lead Maxwell up the grand staircase but my father called out, "We're taking the lift, Jamie."

When we went around behind the staircase I saw that there were actually three "lifts" (or elevators as we called them in Canada) set into the mahogany wall panelling. We stepped into one and the steward said, "C deck, please," to the uniformed boy who was operating it. He didn't look much older than me. We went down one floor and then along a carpeted corridor to our rooms, C-29 and C-31. "It's not like being on a ship at all!" my mother exclaimed as she walked around our suite. "We've never had rooms this large before! Henry, this is marvellous!"

"Just thank the Imperial Bank, my dear," he replied with a small smile.

Suddenly there were several loud blasts from what sounded like huge foghorns.

"That's the whistles giving the all-ashore signal," the steward said. "Must be almost ready for departure."

"We're leaving already?" I asked, throwing my bag down on my bed. "I don't want to miss this!"

"What about Maxwell?" my mother asked.

"I'll take him to the kennels for you, ma'am," the steward replied. Seeing the surprised look on my face, he added, "You can visit him there and take him for walks if you like."

"Oh, all right," I replied, feeling too rushed to argue. "Well, I'm off. I'll see you up top!"

Within seconds I was racing down the corridor, heading for the grand staircase.

CHAPTER TWO

DEPARTURE
Wednesday, April 10, 1912, noon

On reaching the staircase I sprinted up one flight, dodging around the other passengers on the white-tiled steps. One more climb took me to a landing where daylight streamed down from a huge glass dome overhead. At the top of the stairs stood a large clock on the gleaming mahogany wall, surrounded by two carved angels. Both hands pointed to twelve.

Once I reached the boat deck, another deafening blast erupted from the steam whistles high up on the funnels. The gangway we had walked over from the pier had already been removed. One smaller gangway to a lower deck still stood in place for the people leaving the ship. A few minutes later it was swung away too, and not long after that, five men came rushing along the pier waving their arms. They had handkerchiefs tied around their necks and carried cloth satchels.

"Wait, wait!" one of them shouted. "Lower the

gangway!" But there was no response from any-one on the ship.

"Looks like those fellows have missed the boat!" I heard an American man say with a chuckle.

"Poor chaps," said a softer voice beside me. "They've just lost a week's wages. And a stoker doesn't earn much to begin with."

I recognized the Irish accent. It was the same man I'd seen earlier on the gangway, taking photographs.

"Maybe they have enough stokers on board already?" I wondered aloud, then added, "What do stokers do exactly?"

"They shovel coal," the Irishman replied, "into the furnaces for the steam engines. It's hot, dirty work."

Suddenly I felt the ship move as the tugboats started to pull us away from the dock. The stokers who had missed the boat walked away dejectedly. But the other people at the dockside began to cheer and wave, so I waved back at them.

As the huge ship moved down the pier, the crowd onshore followed us. Then flowers started raining down from the upper decks. Some of the pas-sengers were tossing the bouquets they had been given on boarding. I snatched the carnation from my own buttonhole and hurled it over the side.

Suddenly a gust of wind tore off my straw boater and I had to chase it down the deck. I trapped it with my foot and then picked it up and looked at its ugly ribbon done in chocolate brown, blue and yellow stripes, my Winchester house colours.

I don't need this anymore, I decided, and spun it over the railing, watching as it twirled down into the water. Then I took a quick look around, wondering if either of my parents had seen me do this, but, luckily, they were nowhere in sight.

Soon the *Titanic* was approaching two smaller liners that were tied up together at the pier, with crowds of people standing on their decks to get a good view of our departure. All of a sudden I jumped as several short, sharp cracks split the air like gunshots. The mooring cables from one of the liners instantly flew upward and whipped back into the crowd.

"Whoa!" I said. "What was that?"

"Those lines just snapped like threads!" the photographer said. "It must have been suction from our wake. I hope no one was hurt."

Could suction from the *Titanic*'s passing have caused this? I wondered. The ship nearest to us, now untethered, was beginning to swing out in our direction.

"Uh-oh," I said. "That looks like trouble!"

The stern of the liner kept moving outward until it was almost at a right angle to us. The photographer was leaning over the rail with his camera at arm's length. A newspaper headline suddenly popped into my head: *Titanic in Crash While Leaving Port.* I imagined myself telling the boys at my new school in Canada all about it.

"Here comes a smash!" someone said. The Irishman leaned out even farther and clicked away. We both tensed, expecting to feel the crash — but it didn't come. He dashed aft along the deck to get a closer look and I chased after him. We found a spot nearer the stern and leaned over the side. A sudden whoosh of water from one of the *Titanic*'s propellers allowed us to slide by the black hull of the breakaway ship with what seemed like only inches to spare.

"Whew!" I called out. "Looks like we missed her!"

"Well," the Irishman said, grinning, "that was certainly a close shave, as you say in America."

"Yes," I replied, "and we say that in Canada, too."

"You're a Canadian! I do apologize," he said. "It's just that everybody from your side of the herring pond sounds the same to me."

He introduced himself as Frank Browne and said that he was only travelling as far as Queenstown in Ireland, where the *Titanic* would stop tomorrow. "I only have a day and a night on board this marvellous ship," he told me, "so I have to make the most of it. This is my first voyage on an ocean liner."

The *Titanic* had now stopped. As we looked over the side again, we saw that the tugboats were attaching lines to the breakaway steamer in order to tow her away.

"This may hold us up for a bit," said Frank. "But in the meantime," he added, pointing to a steward holding a bugle, "we can have some luncheon."

The steward put the bugle up to his mouth and played a little tune to signal that lunch would soon be served. As I walked back toward the entrance to the grand staircase I ran into my parents.

"Jamie, what happened to your school hat?" my mother asked.

"Oh, the wind blew it off," I replied, telling only half a lie.

My parents decided to take the elevator down to the dining saloon, but I wanted to take the stairs.

"It's four flights down," my father said. "Wait for us in the Palm Room, where we came in this morning."

As I walked down the stairs I could overhear people talking about the near collision and how it seemed rather bad luck for a maiden voyage.

At the bottom of the staircase I stepped onto a deep, red-and-blue-patterned carpet and walked over to some wicker chairs with potted palms around them. A waltz tune was being played by a string trio nearby. The smell of food from the dining saloon made me realize that I was starving. I looked around for my parents and soon noticed them walking from the elevators with two gentlemen. When I waved, the four of them came over. While my father went to see about a table for us, my mother introduced me to one of the men, a Mr. Molson from Montreal.

"Do you make the beer?" I asked him.

"Jamie!" my mother said, flushing slightly. "Mr. Molson is the president of the Molson's Bank!"

"That's true," Mr. Molson replied. "But the Molson brewery is a family business as well. So I suppose you could say I *do* make the beer," he said with a smile.

"But you're a little young for that particular beverage, I think?" asked the other man, whose name, I soon learned, was Major Peuchen. When I told the Major that I was fourteen, he said that he had a son that age back in Toronto.

"I wish he were here," I said. "I haven't seen many people my age on this ship."

"I'm sure you'd be great friends," he replied.

Very soon, though, I began to think that if Major Peuchen's son was as boring as his father, then maybe it was a good thing he wasn't on board. During lunch, the Major talked almost non-stop and it was hard for anyone else to get a word in. When I asked him if he was a major in the army, he told me that he was a volunteer officer with the Queen's Own Rifles, a militia regiment in Toronto. He also had to tell us about how he had accompanied the regiment to the coronation of King George in London last year, and how he had met the king, and how he had ridden in the coronation parade, blah di blah blah.

The Major was obviously a rich man, since he owned his own yacht, as did Mr. Molson, so there was a lot of nautical discussion about this morning's near accident. Major Peuchen's small grey goatee wagged continuously as he told us that he had crossed the Atlantic many times on other White Star ships with our captain, E.J. Smith, and how he thought Smith was much better at flattering rich Americans than he was at navigating a ship.

Mr. Molson interrupted him to say that the captain had made a smart move in firing up the port propeller this morning, since that had allowed us to squeak by the breakaway ship. But Major

Peuchen countered by saying that "in his humble opinion" that particular manoeuvre was likely the harbour pilot's doing . . . Blah di blah blah. Then he told us that Smith had been the captain of the *Titanic*'s sister ship, the *Olympic*, when it had collided with a British warship named the *Hawke* just seven months ago.

"It makes me wonder whether these giant new ships are just too big for 'old E.J.' to handle," he concluded.

"But you don't think we're in any danger, Major, surely?" my mother asked with a smile.

"Oh certainly not, dear lady," laughed the Major. "They say this ship is unsinkable, and I'm sure she is!"

"But what makes her unsinkable?" I asked.

"A double hull," replied Major Peuchen. "The *Titanic* has watertight compartments with doors that can be closed by a switch on the ship's bridge. So if, God forbid, another ship were to ram into us, they could simply seal off the damaged area and prevent the water from spreading throughout the ship. Modern shipbuilding really is a marvel."

The Major could have gone on about this for much longer, but my father changed the subject. As I looked around at the huge dining saloon — the largest room afloat, according to the brochure

— it seemed like we were in a very grand hotel rather than on board a ship. And I was enjoying the food so much that I only half-listened to Major Peuchen's monologue. Our dining steward kept bringing course after course on silver serving trays and I was happy to try everything. I started with what the menu called Hodge Podge soup (and which turned out to have chopped vegetables and beans in it), then I had a plate of Dover sole, followed by grilled lamb chops with baked potatoes — and still had room for some samples from the cheese tray. There was tapioca pudding for dessert, but I didn't care if I ever ate *that* again.

"Hold on, there, Jamie!" my father said as I helped myself to a second pastry. "You'd think they starved you at that school of yours!"

"But they *did!*" I replied as I popped some lemon tart into my mouth.

"Boarding school food, how well I remember," said Mr. Molson, giving me a sympathetic smile.

After lunch my parents said that they were ready for a nap, but I wanted to see what was happening up on deck. During lunch I had felt the engines starting up and the ship beginning to move again. When I stepped onto the boat deck, smoke was pouring out of the first three funnels.

I ran into Rosalie walking on the deck with

another maid that she had met in the servants' dining room. She agreed that the food at lunch was very good and said that her room down on E deck was small but comfortable. I walked forward on the boat deck until I came upon a sign that said *For Use of Crew Only* — I was near the *Titanic*'s bridge. A man stood at the ship's wheel, guiding our course. Through the large windows in front of him I could see the coast of England off to one side and some land appearing in the distance on the other. I wanted to get a closer look at the coastline, so I walked aft to the grand staircase and then down one level.

"Jamie!" a voice called out as I entered the A-deck promenade. "Come and meet Jack!"

I turned and saw Frank Browne, who had just been shooting a photograph of the promenade deck underneath the ship's bridge. There was a boy with him who looked to be about eleven. Frank introduced him as Jack Odell and said that Jack and his family were going on a motoring holiday in Ireland and that he was accompanying them as far as Queenstown.

Jack had a camera hung around his neck and Frank was helping him to take some pictures.

"Here's a good photograph coming up for you, Jack," Frank said, pointing to a round object in the distance.

When we drew closer I saw that what had looked like a channel marker was actually a round stone building rising up out of the water.

"What's *that* supposed to be?" I asked.

"A fort!" said Frank. "There are five of them, built years ago to guard Portsmouth harbour from attack. Portsmouth is a huge naval base."

He told me that we were in a channel called Spithead and that it was here that the king came when there was a big naval review, like the one held last year for the coronation. "His Majesty gets to see hundreds of Britain's mighty ships all lined up," Frank continued. "'Britannia Rules the Waves,' don't you know."

There was an edge to his voice. I wondered if he was one of those people who wanted Ireland to have more independence from Great Britain. After the way I'd been bullied and called Colonial Boy at Winchester, I could understand not wanting to be told what to do by the English.

As we walked forward on the promenade I saw land on the port side and asked what it was.

"That's the Isle of Wight, my boy!" Frank replied with a small chuckle. "Don't they teach you any geography in Canada? I just spoke to an American chap," he continued, "who thought it was the coast of France!"

"Well, I'll bet you don't know where Saskatoon, Saskatchewan, is," I retorted.

"He's got you there, Father!" Jack Odell said as Frank broke into a wide smile.

I wondered why Jack had called Frank "Father." Noting my puzzled look, he said, "I'm not really Father Browne yet, but I will be when I've finished my studies for the priesthood."

"A priest?" I asked, a little taken aback. "Well, uh, I'm sure you'll be a good one." Since we were Anglicans, I hadn't actually met any Catholic priests. And Frank seemed very fun-loving for a priest.

"Come on, boys," he said suddenly. "Let's go and see more of this ship!"

As we entered the grand staircase it seemed like every other passenger on the *Titanic* had had the same idea. There were crowds of people going up and down to each deck. I could hear them ooh-ing and aah-ing about all the splendid rooms they had seen.

"It's just like a floating palace!" one woman said in a plummy English voice.

"It's just like a *floating palace!*" I repeated to Jack in a whispered imitation. He giggled and Frank turned to look at us quizzically, so I called out, "I'd like to see the swimming pool!"

"Very well," replied Frank. "We'll go on down to F deck and work our way up."

We walked down the grand staircase until it ended and then took an elevator down two more decks. The pool was empty, but a steward explained that they would open up a valve tomorrow morning to let sea water into it. I shivered, thinking of all the freezing baths I'd had to take at school. But the Turkish Bath next door looked like a good place to warm up. On entering its main room all three of us just stood and stared, dazzled by the gilded ceiling, brightly patterned tiles and bronze hanging lamps.

"It looks like a sultan's palace!" Frank said.

In another room Jack found a weird contraption called an "electric bath." You sat in it with your head sticking out, and the heat from the light bulbs inside was supposed to be good for your health — at least, that's how the bath attendant explained it.

Nearby was the ship's squash court. Jack and I went to take a look at it, though we both admitted that it wasn't a game we'd ever played. Afterward, we found Frank standing in the corridor, talking with a tall man who also had an Irish accent.

"Come on, boys," Frank said, turning to us. "While we're down here, you should see how the other half lives."

The tall man had rolls of paper under his arm and a pencil placed behind his ear. He waved to a steward, who quickly unlocked a door that let us into the third-class dining saloon. It had white-painted steel walls and long tables with black wooden chairs — quite a contrast to the luxurious room upstairs where we'd just had lunch. We walked through another large room with plain wooden benches in which some third-class passengers were playing cards. The tall Irishman also let us look into an empty third-class cabin that had four bunks and a white sink in the middle. Jack and I both said that we wouldn't mind sleeping in one of those bunks!

"It's a far cry from the comfortable rooms you two are in," said Frank. "Still, it's better than what most of these people have at home."

"And far better than they'd find on any other ship, I'm pleased to say," said the Irishman. "After Queenstown, these cabins will be full of Irish emigrants leaving for America."

"That's the land of hope for our countrymen, I'm afraid," said Frank.

On our way back upstairs Frank told us that our guide had been Thomas Andrews, the *Titanic*'s chief designer.

"He works at Harland and Wolff, a huge ship-building firm in Belfast," Frank explained. "He's on board for this first voyage to make sure everything is up to snuff!"

A few minutes later, Frank suggested that we also take a look into the second-class lounge. Its comfortable sofas and chairs seemed to me every bit as nice as the first-class lounge had been on the *Empress of Britain*. From there we walked to the aft grand staircase, which wasn't quite as fancy as the one farther forward, and had a slightly smaller glass dome overtop it. We took it up three flights to the boat deck and then stood by the railing, looking off into the distance.

"I think we're well past the Isle of Wight by now, so that must be the coast of France ahead," said Frank, pointing forward.

"I've never been to France," I said.

"Well, we won't actually be landing there," replied Frank. "The *Titanic* is too big for the docks in Cherbourg. So we'll anchor offshore and they'll send new passengers out to us in boats."

I was interested to hear about new passengers. Maybe there would be a boy nearer my own age coming on board. With Frank and Jack leaving tomorrow, I really hoped to find someone to have a little fun with on this ship.

CHAPTER THREE

CHERBOURG TO QUEENSTOWN

Wednesday, April 10, 1912, 7:00 p.m.

"Come and meet the Fortunes!" Major Peuchen called to us as we arrived in the Palm Room before dinner. The Fortunes were from Winnipeg, where Mr. Fortune, according to the Major, had "made a fortune to match his name."

His son Charles asked me how I liked the ship so far.

"It's just a *floating palace!*" I said in my imitation English accent.

Charles laughed. "I wish I had a dime for every time I've heard *that* today! But she *is* an amazing ship. Did you see the squash court?"

"Yes," I replied, "although I don't really know how to play."

"I can teach you!" Charles said. "It's really not that hard to learn — as long as you can whack a ball!"

I was surprised that he would want to spend time with a skinny kid like me. Charles was a big, handsome fellow who would be going to McGill

University in the fall. Talking to him reminded me just how friendly Canadians can be. He mentioned that he had played on the hockey team at Bishop's College School in Lennoxville.

"That's *my* new school!" I replied. "I'm going there in September."

"You'll love it!" said Charles, flashing his big grin. "It has acres of land all around it — and lakes right nearby."

I instantly wondered if freezing skinny dips were required and told Charles about the cold baths at Winchester. He laughed and said that there were plenty of hot showers at Bishop's. Charles, his parents and three older sisters were on their way home after doing a grand tour of Europe — including a trip down the Nile in Egypt. When Charles described how very hot it had been in Cairo, he added, "It's a good thing Father brought along his winter coat!" His sisters smiled at this. It turned out that there was a running family joke about the huge buffalo coat that Mr. Fortune had insisted on bringing with him. But Mr. Fortune just grinned and replied that you never knew when you'd need a warm coat.

It would have been fun to sit with the Fortunes at dinner, but my father had already signed us up to share a table with Major Peuchen and Mr. Molson for the whole voyage.

"For the *whole* trip?" I whispered to my mother when I heard this, but she quickly said "Shhh" and rolled her eyes. Luckily, Major Peuchen didn't talk quite as much at dinner as he had at lunch, so Mr. Molson was able to tell us about his yacht, the *Alcyone*, which he said was seventy-five feet long. I whistled at this, which drew a frown from my father.

Mr. Molson's family also owned a shipping company and he told us how he had once been on a ship in the St. Lawrence River when it was rammed by a coal freighter.

"I was in bed when it happened," he said. "I managed to throw on a shirt and pair of trousers before I jumped through my stateroom window into the river."

"I'll bet that was cold!" I said.

"Like ice!" he replied. "But luckily I was picked up by a lifeboat, or else I might not be here to tell the tale."

The food at dinner was fancier than it had been at lunch. The menu offered chicken à la this and duck à la that. It was all delicious, though, and I enjoyed listening to Mr. Molson's stories.

As we left the dining saloon, I noticed that some of the Cherbourg passengers who had just come on board were being ushered to their rooms by the chief steward and his staff. A boy about my age was walking by with his family, so I gave him a small wave and he nodded back.

Back up on deck, I saw a few passengers leaving the ship via a gangway from D deck to the tender waiting below. One was wheeling a bicycle and another carried a canary in a cage. I watched the tender pull away from the side of the liner and continue around the breakwater toward the lights of Cherbourg. The glowing portholes of the *Titanic* reflected in the water and I thought what a beautiful sight she must be for the people on shore. The deep-toned whistles atop the funnels suddenly blew three times, followed by the rattle of the anchors being raised and the rumble of the engines starting up. Before long the lights of Cherbourg became smaller and smaller, until they finally disappeared into the darkness behind our wake.

* * *

I awoke early the next morning to the thrumming sound of the engines. When I looked out the porthole a pink sky lit the horizon and I decided to go out on deck before my parents were up. Perhaps I could get my first look at the coast of Ireland.

"Good morning to you, Jamie!" Frank Browne called out when I reached the boat deck. He was there with his camera and said he'd just taken a beautiful shot of the sunrise.

"Have you seen the coast of Ireland yet?" I asked.

"It'll be a while before we see that, I expect," he replied. "I did spot something in the distance that I think was Land's End."

Even though my English geography wasn't perfect, I knew that Land's End was at the tip of Cornwall, on the southwest coast of England. I hadn't realized we would go by there on our way to Ireland.

"I thought that I might take a snap inside the Marconi room, if they'll let me," Frank said as he walked toward a room on the boat deck that had wires hanging above its roof. "It's amazing to think they can send wireless messages from the middle of the ocean nowadays."

He knocked on the door and we walked into a tiny room where a wireless operator was sitting at a desk against a wall that had two clocks on it, as well as boxes with dials and switches. He had earphones on and was using a small lever on the desk to tap out messages in Morse code.

"Can't talk — too busy," he said, glancing briefly up at us. I was surprised to see how young he looked, perhaps only four or five years older than me.

"Can I take a quick photo?" Frank asked. The man nodded.

While Frank took his shot there was a rattle from one of the brass tubes that curved down from the ceiling against the wall. Then a small cylinder popped out from the horn-shaped end of the tube and landed in a tray on the desk.

"Another one!" said the operator as he flipped open the end of the cylinder and pulled out a rolled-up piece of paper. "You leave your message at the enquiry office," he told us, glancing briefly our way, "and they shoot 'em up 'ere through this tube."

Just then another wireless operator, who seemed to be the boss, opened a door and glared at us. Behind him I could see a second small room filled with equipment. Frank and I quickly backed out the entry door onto the boat deck.

"Well, I suppose passengers aren't supposed to just drop in," Frank remarked as we walked away. "But that pneumatic tube system is remarkable! Works on compressed air, I believe."

I'd seen one in a department store in Montreal, and remembered being amazed when our receipt and some change had come rattling down the pneumatic tube after my mother had bought me new shoes.

Frank checked his watch. "I think it's time for breakfast," he said. He headed toward the grand staircase while I made my way back to our state-room.

"Up early, I see," said my father when I got there. He was already dressed and waiting for my mother.

As we walked into the dining saloon I noticed that some people were having fish for breakfast, which made my stomach flip. I wrinkled my nose at the herring and haddock on offer and chose fresh fruit and Quaker oats instead, followed by a tomato omelette and raisin scones with marmalade.

As soon as I was finished I asked my father if I could take Maxwell for a walk.

"The kennels are on the boat deck, but I'm not sure exactly where," he said. "I'll come with you after breakfast if you like."

I said I'd be fine on my own and headed off to find Max. When I reached the boat deck the sun broke through the clouds. I strolled along beside the railing, listening for the sound of barking from the kennels. Then I saw a man in a white apron carrying a bucket of what looked like bones. I followed him to just behind the fourth funnel, where he opened a door and the sounds of yips and barks floated out on the sea air. Inside were rows of cages filled with many different kinds of dogs. Maxwell noticed me immediately and began jumping up and yelping. As the man in the white apron put down his bucket of bones, the dogs started barking even more loudly.

"One 'a them yours?" the man asked in a broad Yorkshire accent.

"Yes, that one there," I yelled above the din, pointing to Maxwell. "I'd like to take him for a walk."

"You'll 'ave to ask the steward," he said. "I'm just the ship's butcher. I bring 'em bones and scraps from the galley."

The steward soon arrived and unlocked Max's cage. I managed to snap his leash onto his collar just as he made a dash for the door. He was so excited to be out of the kennel, he pulled me out into the sunshine and I had to run to keep up. I eventually stopped him by the portside railing to see if there was any sight of land.

"An Airedale!" I suddenly heard a voice say. "Hello, pup, hello!"

A boy was kneeling down beside Max, patting him and getting licked all over his face. "We have an Airedale back home," he said. "What's yours called?"

"Maxwell," I said, "or just Max. He answers to both."

"Maxwell, Maxwell, Maxmaxmax," the boy went

on as he buried his face in Maxwell's neck. "You're a very good dog, a very good dog, yes you are!"

I realized that this was the same boy I'd seen in the Palm Room last night.

"What's your dog's name?" I asked.

"We call him Otsie," he replied.

"Otsie?" I asked, raising my eyebrows.

"Well, we got him near our summer place on Lake Otsego, so my sister said we should call him after the lake. I thought it was a dumb name, but when you shorten it to Otsie, it's okay. And we're all used to it by now!" he explained.

"I'm Jamie Laidlaw," I said, "from Montreal."

"Jamie Canuck!" he said, standing up and shaking my hand. "I'm John Ryerson."

"Johnnie the Yank!" I replied, and he grinned.

"Do you speak French?" he asked.

"Only a little," I said.

"Better than me!" he said with a laugh. "I can't speak any. My mother has a French maid named Victorine and I can't make out a word she says."

Suddenly Johnnie grabbed Max's leash and raced off down the deck with him, yahoo-ing loudly.

"Hey!" I yelled, chasing after him. I found him catching his breath near one of the lifeboats.

"Just thought I'd put Max through his paces," he said with a grin.

"Yankee dog thief!" I said, punching his arm.

He tapped me back on the shoulder and said, "Aww, you Canucks just have to learn to keep up!"

"Look," I said, pointing over the rail, "Land ho!" There was just the faintest trace of some hills in the distance.

"The Emerald Isle," said Johnnie. "Too bad we're not landing there. I've never been to Ireland."

Suddenly Max started barking and pulling on his leash. He had spotted another dog — an Airedale walking alongside a tall man with a large black moustache. The man brought his dog over and the two Airedales began sniffing each other.

"You boys have good taste in dogs," the man said. "What's his name?"

"Maxwell," I replied.

"Kitty, meet Maxwell," the tall man said to his dog just as the two Airedales began growling at each other and raising their hackles. It looked like a fight was about to start, so the man pulled on Kitty's leash and quickly moved on down the deck.

"You know who that was?" Johnnie asked me after he'd left.

I shook my head.

"John Jacob Astor," he said.

I shook my head again.

"The Waldorf-Astoria Hotel, you've heard of *that?*" he asked. This time I nodded.

"Well, he *owns* it," Johnnie continued, "and most of New York City as well. My father says he's America's richest man."

"Well, we have Canada's richest man at our table," I replied. "Mr. Molson has his own yacht and owns a bank and also Molson's beer — maybe you've heard of that?"

"They served beer at lunch yesterday," Johnnie said. "I asked for some but the steward said I was too young."

"My father would have a fit if he caught me drinking beer," I said. "At my school in England, some boys were expelled for going to a pub. English boarding schools are very strict. I'm glad to be out of there."

"Did you have to play cricket?" he asked.

"Yes, but I could never make sense of it," I replied. "Baseball seems a much better game to me."

When I asked him where he went to school in the States, he looked down and hesitated a little before saying, "Well, umm, I have a tutor, Miss Bowen. But only because we've been travelling abroad. She's actually on board with us."

I thought having a tutor and being taught at

home would be even worse than being sent to an English boarding school, so I decided to change the subject by suggesting we take Maxwell back to the kennels. After we had put Max back in his cage and admired the other dogs we went down one level to the A-deck promenade. Its enclosed windows made it a little warmer for sitting on deck chairs.

Before long, we came closer to the Irish coast and I could see jagged cliffs with waves crashing against them. There were sandy coves and looming headlands too, with green hills shrouded in mist.

"Look, there's a castle," I said, pointing to a ruin on a hilltop.

After a while, we felt the *Titanic* slowing down. I asked a crewman standing nearby if we were arriving at Queenstown.

"We're not too far away," he replied, "but we 'ave to pick up the 'arbour pilot. Then we anchor off Roche's Point."

I didn't quite understand what he was saying at first because he had such a strong accent. But he eventually explained that the harbour pilot would help guide the ship toward Queenstown, where it would anchor outside the harbour.

Johnnie and I watched the pilot come on board and later saw the lighthouse on Roche's Point near the mouth of Queenstown harbour. I suggested to Johnnie that we have an early lunch and took him down to our stateroom to ask my parents if he could sit at our table.

"I have a better idea," my mother said. "I'll ring for the steward and ask him to bring you boys some sandwiches."

I quickly agreed with her, because we didn't want to waste a lot of time in the dining saloon. And I didn't want Major Peuchen to pepper Johnnie with questions about his family. It seemed as if Johnnie's family was really rich, so the Major would want to know all about them.

After we had eaten the sandwiches, Johnnie and I put on our coats and hurried back up to the boat deck. A tender down below had piles of mailbags on it, along with the people who were waiting to come on board. One of them was playing the bagpipes on the tender's deck.

A second tender was approaching from the harbour with smoke belching out of its single funnel. Soon there were crowds of people up on deck watching as the mailbags were unloaded and the arriving passengers were brought aboard through a lower gangway. Some vendors from Queenstown came on board too, and held up handmade Irish lace for passengers to purchase. I noticed Mr. Astor bargaining with one woman and then pulling out a wad of bills to buy something.

When I saw the last tender being loaded I suggested to Johnnie that we head down to D deck so I could say goodbye to Frank Browne and Jack Odell. We caught up with Frank and the Odells in the Palm Room. He shook my hand, wished me well and said that he would never forget his two days on board this beautiful ship. Johnnie and I went back up onto the boat deck to wave him and the Odells off. I smiled when I saw that Frank was still shooting photos as he departed.

Then came the clanking of the anchor being raised. Over that din came some startled shrieks. People were pointing at the fourth funnel. Johnnie and I looked up and began to laugh. A man with a soot-blackened face was peering out from the top of it. I realized that he was just one of the stokers who had climbed up a ladder inside the funnel to get some fresh air. Obviously some people didn't know that the fourth funnel was a dummy just used for ventilation.

"He gave me *such* a fright! I thought it was the Devil himself!" said one woman in a very proper English accent. This made us both burst out laughing once again. "I thought it was the *Devil* himself!" would become a favourite laugh line for Johnnie and me.

Smoke started belching out of the funnels as the *Titanic* got underway and began steaming along the south coast of Ireland. Johnnie and I walked the decks with Maxwell as we admired the passing scenery. After a few hours the coastline ended and we swung past a tall white lighthouse on a small rocky outcrop that marked the southern tip of Ireland. From there the ship turned westward to head out across the Atlantic. The sun was edging lower on the horizon when I heard the sound of the bagpipes again and spied the piper from Queenstown standing at the *Titanic*'s stern. As the Irish coastline retreated in the distance, he saluted the homeland he might never see again with a mournful dirge. Overhead, seagulls wheeled in the air as the green hills slowly became ever smaller, until they finally disappeared in the mist.

CHAPTER FOUR

AT SEA
Saturday, April 13, 1912

By Saturday, Johnnie and I were getting a little bored on the *Titanic*. It seemed like we had done everything there was to do on the ship. We had given Maxwell regular walks around the boat deck. We had tried playing deck shuffleboard, but neither of us knew the rules of the game. The gym instructor had kicked us out of the gymnasium on Friday morning for fooling around on the exercise machines. I had tried the stationary bike while Johnnie straddled the mechanical camel — a crazy contraption which gave you a wobbly ride that was supposed to be good for your liver. Johnnie had bounced around on it pretending to be an Arab sheik barking out commands to a camel. I thought it was hilarious, but the gym instructor, a short Scotsman who took his job very seriously, turned red in the face and told us to leave. So we went down and sweated in the Turkish Bath and relaxed on the loungers in the room with the coloured tiles and the bronze lamps. Charles

Fortune and his father came in after their squash game and Charles joined us for a plunge in the swimming pool. The sea water had been heated a little, so it wasn't icy cold.

My parents seemed perfectly happy just sitting and reading in the first-class lounge and taking walks on deck. Mother was particularly glad that the weather was pleasant and the ocean so calm, since she had suffered from seasickness during our trip over on the *Empress of Britain*. Each day at noon the distance we had travelled was posted near the purser's office and people would gather around to check on our progress. At lunch on Friday, Major Peuchen had said that J. Bruce Ismay, the managing director of the White Star Line, told him that the *Titanic* was performing even better than the *Olympic* had on her maiden voyage.

* * *

After lunch on Saturday I ran into Johnnie in the Palm Room just as he was stuffing something wrapped in a napkin into his pocket.

"Snacks for later?" I asked.

"Just getting a little food for my rat," he replied.

"For your *what?*" I asked.

"My rat," he repeated, as if everybody had one. "Want to see him?"

"Sure," I said, thinking that Johnnie was more full of surprises than just about anyone I'd ever met.

"This will have to be our secret," he whispered as we went into his room, "because my parents don't know about my rat. Neither does Miss Bowen. Victorine knows, because she was with me when I bought it at a market in Paris. But she promised she wouldn't tell."

From under his bed, Johnnie pulled out a small wire cage. When he took the cloth cover off, sure enough, there, sitting calmly, was a large white rat with a long tail. Johnnie poured some water into the little bowl in the cage.

"Do you have a name for him?" I asked.

"I just call him Rat," Johnnie replied, as he fed him lettuce from his hand.

The rat's pointed nose and fat little face suddenly gave me an idea.

"Sykes!" I said. "We should call him Sykes. He looks just like a prefect I hated at school."

"We can call him Sykes, if you like," Johnnie replied as the rat nibbled lettuce from his hand.

"Do you think Sykes would like to see the sea?" I asked.

"I don't think he's ever seen the sea," Johnnie said with a grin. "He probably doesn't even know he's on a boat. Let's take him for a walk. I'll just keep him in my pocket till we're clear of my family."

As we walked along the A-deck promenade toward the bow, Johnnie kept his hand in his pocket to cover any telltale wriggling.

"Oh, ugh!" he yelped as we approached the forward railing. "Sykes just *pooped* on my hand!"

"Oh no," I said, trying not to laugh as I pulled out my handkerchief. "Here, clean it off with this."

As Johnnie wiped his hand there was suddenly a yipping sound behind us. It was Mr. Astor's dog, scratching at Johnnie's leg while Mr. Astor pulled back on her leash. Kitty obviously smelled a rat. All of a sudden, Sykes popped out of Johnnie's pocket, hit the deck and scurried along beside the railing. Johnnie took off in pursuit.

"Wait!" I called out and ran after him, leaving a puzzled Mr. Astor behind to restrain Kitty. Sykes was already heading down the stairs to the forward well deck. He crawled underneath a metal gate at the top of the steps. Johnnie vaulted over the gate and then stumbled and rolled down the stairway onto the deck below.

A sign on the gate said *For Use of Crew Only* but I decided to clamber over it anyway. When I reached the well deck I found Johnnie prowling around the base of one of the giant cargo cranes. Nearby was a hatch covered with canvas. If Sykes gets under there, I thought, he'll be gone forever.

"There he is!" Johnnie shouted, pointing forward. Sykes was climbing a set of steps that led up to the forecastle deck, where the foremast stood. On the deck beneath it the anchor chains were stretched out beside huge iron bollards. I knew we'd be in big trouble if we went up there, but Johnnie was already bounding up the stairs, so I followed.

"He could be *anywhere* up here," I said when I got to the top of the steps. But Johnnie was already beginning to climb up onto one of the big round windlasses that raised the anchor chains, to get a higher view.

"I don't think you should — " I began, but a loud bellow drowned me out. A man in a blue officer's uniform was charging across the well deck.

"Down!" he yelled. "Get down from there! This instant!"

Johnnie quickly jumped back onto the deck. We both turned to face the officer. I dreaded what was coming.

"What do you lads think you're *playing* at?" the officer roared.

I felt my face burning.

"I was looking for my, uh, pet," Johnnie said coolly.

"Your pet?" the officer bellowed. "What *kind* of pet?"

"Well, it's a . . . a . . . "

"A hamster," I said.

"A *hamster?*" the officer roared. "Have you taken leave of your senses, boys? You climbed up here to look for a *hamster?* You could have been killed!"

"We're very sorry!" I blurted out. "We didn't know — "

"Come with me," he ordered. "I've a good mind to take you both to the captain."

Johnnie kept craning his head to look for Sykes as we walked down the stairs to the well deck with the officer behind us. He made us walk up another three decks to the bridge.

"Wait here," he said after we reached the door to the wheelhouse.

I could hear him inside, conferring with another officer.

Soon he came out. "We'll have a word with your parents," he said.

We went first to the Ryerson cabins. When the officer knocked on one of the doors, a woman I supposed was Johnnie's tutor, Miss Bowen, answered.

"Good afternoon, ma'am, I'm Second Officer Lightoller. I caught this young scamp on top of a windlass just now," he said. "Young fool had no business at all being on the fo'c'sle deck — it's a restricted area. Could have injured himself."

"Oh, John, how *could* you?" Miss Bowen said. "How could you be so foolish? And at such a time, too. Your poor mother."

Johnnie stared down at his shoes.

"I'll leave him in your hands, ma'am," Officer Lightoller said, tipping his cap to Miss Bowen as Johnnie went inside.

As we walked toward our stateroom, I saw my parents in the corridor, returning from a walk on deck. What rotten luck! I'd been hoping they might be in the lounge. My father noticed Officer Lightoller and immediately sensed that something was up.

"Good afternoon, officer," he called out. "I see you have my son with you. Anything the matter?"

"Afternoon, sir," Lightoller replied. "We found him and another lad in a restricted area."

"I see," said my father. "Up to some mischief, were they?"

"Well," Lightoller continued, "I caught the other lad clambering onto a windlass on the fo'c'sle deck."

"Good heavens, Jamie," my mother snapped. "Have you no sense at all?"

"Very well, officer," my father said, in a steady

voice designed to calm my mother. "Thank you for returning him to us. We'll see that this doesn't happen again."

He motioned me into the cabin.

"Who were you with?" my mother demanded once we were inside our suite.

"Johnnie," I replied.

"The Ryerson boy? Oh, Jamie, how *could* you!" she said, becoming even more agitated. "His poor mother, as if she didn't have enough to bear already!"

"What's wrong with his mother?" I asked.

"Didn't he tell you? The family is in mourning!" she replied. She said that Johnnie's eldest brother was killed in a motoring accident while on Easter break from Yale. "The Ryersons got word in Paris and are going home for the funeral."

"Don't tell me you didn't notice his father wearing a black arm band," my father said.

"I haven't really met either of his parents," I replied.

"Well, they're keeping to themselves, of course," my mother said. "But people will be talking about this. They'll blame us, I know it."

"Now, now, my dear — " my father began.

But my mother was far from done with me. "That American boy likely doesn't know any better," she snapped. "But you've been to a *proper* English school!"

My father turned to me and said that I'd upset my mother very badly, which I knew was a cardinal sin. From now on I was "confined to barracks," as he put it, using one of his old British army terms. "You are not to leave this room for the rest of the voyage unless you're with us," he said as he ushered my mother into their room and closed the door.

I threw myself onto the bed and punched my pillow. Stuck in this room or tied to my parents for the rest of the trip! It was too awful to think about! And I'd probably never see Johnnie again. I wondered why he hadn't told me about his brother. I felt guilty about suggesting we take Sykes for a walk. Now Johnnie had lost his pet, and it was really my fault.

Eventually I fell asleep and woke up to the sound of the bugler playing out on deck. Moments later I heard my parents stirring in the other room as they began to dress for dinner. I was glad that my school blazer and tie were good enough for me to wear in the dining saloon, and that I didn't have to wear a tuxedo like my father did.

"Time to get dressed," my father said, popping his head out the door.

"I'm not going," I muttered.

"Suit yourself," he replied. "But you're not to leave the cabin."

My mother's perfume wafted toward me as they came out of their room all dressed up. Mother even had her diamonds on and a small tiara in her hair. She seemed almost relieved that I wasn't going down to the dining saloon, so I knew I really was in disgrace. After they left, I could hear Rosalie tidying up in their room. She must have come up to help my mother get dressed for dinner.

"I 'ear you 'ave been a naughty boy," she said as she came through into my room.

"That's what they tell me," I sighed.

"I try to tell your mother," she said. "I tell her it's no big thing, but you know your mother. I should not be saying this, but, you know, she care too much what people think. And there are so many rich people on this ship."

"Yes," I said. "But it's not like she's going to see any of them again once we're home."

Rosalie turned toward the door, promising to bring some dinner up for me.

She returned about half an hour later with a plate of food. "Now I go and finish my dinner," she said as she left.

I ate quickly and then looked at my watch. It would be at least an hour before my parents finished their dinner and then had coffee while they listened to the orchestra. That would give me some time. I cracked open the door and checked out the corridor. It was empty, so I walked along it to the Ryerson cabins, on the other side of the ship. I crept up to Johnnie's room and put my ear to the door. All was quiet inside. I tapped on the door and then ducked around a corner. A few minutes later Johnnie stuck his head out.

"Hey, Johnnie," I whispered. "Are you alone?"

"Coast is clear," he said, "come on in."

I stepped into his room and he shut the door.

"I am so-o-o sorry — " I began, but he interrupted me.

"Sorry about what?"

"About getting us into trouble," I replied.

"Oh *that*," he said. "I wouldn't worry about *that*. Miss Bowen hasn't told my parents about it because she doesn't want to upset them. I got a tongue-lashing from my sisters, but I couldn't care less about that. And now I get to eat in my room, which is much better anyway. Here, have a sandwich," he said, pointing to a tray on the washstand.

"Well, I'm sorry about your brother," I said. "I didn't know about him."

"Yes," Johnnie said, his face darkening, "it's very sad. And I think about him a lot. I think about him flying out of that car and hitting a fence — which is what happened. I just hope he died quickly."

He looked up. "But I just can't be sad *all* the time, you know? My mother cries all day long. My sisters mope around. I just needed to have some fun. That's why I didn't tell you about him."

"I feel bad that we lost Sykes. Taking him out on deck was my stupid idea," I said.

"Oh, don't worry." He shrugged. "Say, do *all* Canucks apologize a lot?"

"Maybe we do," I said with a small smile. "But I better get back to my cell before they realize I've escaped."

"Okay," said Johnnie, "you're a pal. Let me check that no snoops are about."

He poked his head out the door and then gestured to me. I scurried down the corridor and across to the other side of the ship and into my room. Only minutes later I heard my parents' voices outside and threw the covers over my head, pretending to be asleep. Once they had gone into their room and all was quiet, I got up and brushed my teeth, put on my pyjamas and got back into bed. Soon I was sound asleep.

CHAPTER FIVE
A Quiet Sunday
Sunday, April 14, 1912

"Let's take Max for a turn around the deck, shall we?" my father suggested after breakfast on Sunday morning.

"Remember, we're attending the church service at half-past ten, Henry," my mother added.

I stifled a sigh. Obviously a very long, boring day lay ahead for me. My parents seemed determined not to let me out of their sight. Max, at least, was excited to see me and began yelping and scratching at his cage door the moment my father and I walked into the kennels. I knelt down and fed him a few sausages that I'd wrapped in a napkin at breakfast. Once I got him out on deck, Max pulled ahead on his leash, so I sped up and then broke into a run behind him, waving over my shoulder to my father, and happy to have a few minutes of freedom. Max slowed down a little as we reached the second funnel. The ocean was still very calm, with only small waves and almost no whitecaps.

The *Titanic* seemed to be making good time and I wondered if today's posted mileage would be greater than yesterday's.

I kept hoping I might see Johnnie on deck, but when there was no sign of him I decided to walk back and find my father. I spotted him standing in a small group by the railing, listening to a short, stubby man who was gesturing with a short, stubby cigar. He had a commanding presence, even though his full beard made him look like he had no neck.

"Mr. Hays, this is my son, James," my father said, but Mr. Hays merely nodded at me and carried on talking. "Yes, the Chateâu is going to be like no hotel Ottawa has ever seen before. I'd say it will outdo even the *Titanic* for luxury, wouldn't you agree, Payne?" he asked, turning to a young man next to him.

"Oh, yes sir," Payne replied.

"We're naming it after Laurier, you know," Mr. Hays stated proudly and my father nodded his approval — he had always been a staunch supporter of Prime Minister Wilfrid Laurier.

"There will be a grand opening ceremony when we get back," Mr. Hays continued, "and my sculptor friend, Monsieur Chevré here," he said, pointing to a third man standing beside the railing, "will see his very fine bust of Laurier installed in the lobby."

Monsieur Chevré, who had been looking out to sea while smoking a smelly French cigarette, turned and gave us a small bow. He looked every bit the French *artiste* with his small goatee and large felt hat.

"Excellent!" said my father. He glanced at his watch and added, "Well, I'm afraid we must join my wife for the Sunday service." We all shook hands and my father and I walked Maxwell back to the kennels.

"You knew Mr. Hays already?" I asked.

"Yes. Hays is the president of the Grand Trunk Railway," he replied as we walked toward the staircase entrance. "A very important account for the bank. That young assistant of his, Vivian Payne, lost his father as a boy. Hays has more or less adopted him."

I was glad I didn't have to work for Mr. Hays. And I was also glad that my name wasn't Vivian!

When we returned to our stateroom, my mother was already dressed for church and waiting for us. I put on my school tie and blazer and followed my parents to the dining saloon. A good number of people were seated in the chairs that had been set up in the centre of the room. Captain Smith was already standing in front of a lectern with the piano behind him. We took seats off to one side near the back.

I looked around for Johnnie and his family and saw them across the room in the second row. He and his father were both wearing black arm bands and his sisters and Miss Bowen were all in black. So was his mother, who had a black veil drawn over her face.

Captain Smith looked very impressive with his white beard and his blue uniform with brass buttons and gold stripes on the sleeves. He welcomed us all on behalf of the White Star Line and then read the service from a book on the lectern. It wasn't too different from the Anglican chapel services we'd had at school, except that there was no boys' choir singing in Latin. We all stood when the pianist played the first few bars of each hymn. The last one was O God Our Help in Ages Past. As I was singing the line about "our shelter from the stormy blast," I suddenly spied something moving near the wall. I put the hymnal up over my face and turned my head to have a closer look. The tables had been moved to the side of the room, and there was definitely something moving underneath them. Then a small white face stuck its pointed nose around a table leg.

Yikes! It's Sykes! I thought as my heart began to pound. How could I catch him without causing a scene? Then I saw that a steward had noticed him too. As the steward started to move toward the table, Sykes darted away underneath it. I was afraid one of the ladies might see him and let out a scream. But just then the service ended and people started milling about and talking. While my parents chatted with the Fortunes, I pushed my way over to the Ryersons. I grabbed Johnnie by the wrist and whispered, "Sykes! Over by the wall!" and pointed my head to where I'd seen him. Johnnie's eyes widened and he gave me a small nod. Miss Bowen glared at me, so I beat a hasty retreat back to my parents before my absence was noticed.

When we returned to the dining saloon at lunchtime, I glanced around for any sign of Sykes, but saw nothing. During lunch, Major Peuchen told us that he had sent a wireless message to his wife in Toronto and that it was "a modern marvel" to be able to do that from a ship at sea. "It wasn't cheap, so I expect it's a very profitable racket for the Marconi company," he added.

"Oh, Henry," said my mother. "We must send one to Arthur! 'Greetings from *Titanic* in mid-Atlantic' or something like that!"

"It's easy!" I said. "You just give your message to the enquiry office and it goes up through a pneu-matic tube and pops out in the Marconi room."

"Jamie!" my mother said, "How do you *know* all this?"

"I was there!" I replied casually. "With Father Browne, when he was taking a photograph of the Marconi room. Before he got off in Queenstown."

"Well, you have been getting around," my father observed, with a tinge of disapproval in his voice. But after lunch he and I walked up to C deck to send a wireless message to my brother. Arthur was eight years older than me and was already working for the Imperial Bank in Montreal. I knew my father was pleased about him choosing banking as a career.

As we approached the purser's office we saw a number of people looking at the new posting of the distance we had travelled so far.

I checked the notice board. "It says we've gone five hundred and forty-six nautical miles since noon on Saturday," I announced to my father. "That's even better than the five hundred and nineteen we did yesterday!"

He nodded and we went inside the purser's office and found the window for the enquiry office. There was a charge of twelve shillings and sixpence for sending a wireless message of up to ten words, and ninepence for every word beyond that, so my father kept it brief: *Greetings from Titanic. In NY Wed. Arrive Montreal Thurs. Father.*

"Let's go up on deck again," I said after we had finished. I hoped there might be a chance of running into Johnnie there. I also thought I might look in on the Marconi room and possibly see our message pop out from the pneumatic tube.

As we walked forward, I hurried toward the Marconi room door. "Let's see if they have our message!" I said.

"Hold on, Jamie. I don't think — " my father started to say, but I'd already begun to open the door. At the desk inside was the same young operator Frank Browne had photographed.

"Not now, son! Too busy!" he called out sharply. I glimpsed a large number of messages piled up on his desk. Many more cylinders sat in the tray below the pneumatic tube.

"'Nother ice message!" I heard him call to his boss as I shut the door.

"They're too busy," I said to my father.

"Yes, I'm not surprised," he said, clearly disapproving of me having gone in there.

"What's an ice message?" I asked him.

"Ice message?" he replied, raising his eyebrows. "That's likely from another ship telling us that there are icebergs ahead. You often see them on spring crossings."

"An iceberg!" I said. "I'd love to see an iceberg. Have you ever seen one?"

"Oh, once or twice," he responded. "But never up close."

Now I really hoped to run into Johnnie so I could tell him that we might be seeing icebergs. That would be something to get excited about. I thought we might give Max another walk on deck, but we soon spotted the steward from the kennels with a fistful of leashes in each hand as he walked eight dogs along the deck. Max was among them, along with a handsome English bulldog and a tiny King Charles spaniel.

It had turned colder, and my father suggested that we go back down to the stateroom. I agreed, as I was starting to shiver. I continued reading my book, *Captains Courageous,* till later in the afternoon, when my mother suggested that we all have tea in the Café Parisien.

"We haven't been there yet and it looks so charming," she said, "just like a sidewalk café in Paris. Your father and I are dining late this evening," she added. "In the Ritz restaurant with the Fortunes, so tea will sustain us till then. You can have something in the room tonight, if you'd like."

The thought of sitting at our usual table listening to Major Peuchen ramble on and on didn't thrill me, so I nodded in approval. Maybe I could sneak out at dinnertime to find Johnnie and tell him about the icebergs.

As we approached the entrance to the Café Parisien we heard raised voices and laughter and soon saw Charles Fortune and two of his sisters at the door, along with another young man. When they noticed us, Ethel Fortune cried, "We just saw a mouse in there, can you believe it?"

"But Will chased it," added Alice Fortune, turning to the young man beside her.

"It wasn't a mouse, I tell you. It was a *rat,* a white rat!" he replied.

"With a long, slimy tail!" Charles added, which made his sisters shriek with mock horror.

"Good afternoon," my father said to the Fortunes in an unruffled voice. "Glad to see you're all enjoying yourselves." No one noticed that I'd flushed crimson at the mention of the white rat.

"William Sloper seems very keen on Alice Fortune," my mother said to my father after we were seated at one of the round tables in the café. "I gather they met on the ship on the way over and he booked on the *Titanic* just to be near her."

"Hmm, yes," said my father as he looked over the menu card.

"Mind you, he lives in Connecticut," my mother continued, "which is a long way from Winnipeg . . . "

I wasn't paying much attention to their conversation, as I was eyeing the cakes and pastries on the dessert table. They all looked good to me, but I was afraid they might be irresistible to Sykes, if he was still nearby. I suddenly imagined a big white rat gorging himself on the cakes and all the screaming that would follow, which made me smile.

"You look happy, Jamie," my mother said.

"Oh, I'm just thinking about those cakes," I replied.

The Café Parisien had white trellises along the walls with ivy growing up them. Through the arched windows I could see the ocean going by and it seemed as if we were going faster.

"I think we've speeded up," I said to my father.

"Yes," he said, looking out the window. "They may have lit another boiler."

"I think we'll have a lovely sunset tonight," my mother said, looking out at the horizon.

"I doubt many will want to go out on deck to see it," my father replied. "The temperature seems to be plummeting."

After we had drunk our tea and I had fully gorged myself on cream buns and a slice of Eccles cake, my mother insisted we take a look at the Ritz restaurant, since it was right beside the café. It was very ritzy indeed, with carved pillars and polished wooden panelling with lots of shiny gold decoration on it. The staff were setting up the tables for dinner and putting small vases of flowers on the white tablecloths.

"This looks just lovely, Henry," my mother said. "I'm so glad the Fortunes invited us to dine here."

I was equally glad that this dinner would give me an evening to myself. And since I was feeling stuffed from all I'd eaten in the café, I wouldn't need to worry about food for a while. As we came to the staircase I said to my father. "I'll just look in on Max for a minute."

"We-e-ll, all right," he replied, clearly reluctant to let me go off on my own. "But don't be long."

It was very cold up on the boat deck and only one or two other people were out there to see the sky begin to turn pink. There were no stewards in the kennel area either, so I just spent a few minutes with Max before I walked forward on the boat deck and looked down toward the forecastle deck where Johnnie and I had been nabbed by Officer Lightoller. Up in the crow's nest high on the mast I thought I could see the lookout on duty, scanning the horizon for any icebergs ahead. I headed back to the staircase and went down to B deck. Instead of turning toward our stateroom, however, I suddenly decided to look in on Johnnie. I knocked on his door and Miss Bowen answered.

"Is John here?" I asked.

She fetched him, but stood only a few feet away from the door so she could listen to our conversation.

"My parents are dining in the Ritz restaurant tonight," I said.

"We're all in the dining saloon," he replied. "Except for my mother and Emily — that's my sister — who's going to keep her company in the room."

"They say we might be seeing icebergs soon," I said.

"So I've heard," he replied. "I'd love to see one up close!"

"Our friend Sykes was in the café for tea today," I added.

"Was he?" Johnnie's eyebrows shot up. "He does get around. I heard he was trying out the machines in the gym."

"The mechanical camel is his favourite, I believe," I said.

"Yes, well, the rowing machine is too hard for his skinny arms," he added, managing to keep a straight face.

I was finding it a challenge not to laugh, so

I quickly waved goodbye and went back to our stateroom. Rosalie was there, preparing to get my mother dressed for the evening. She asked what I was doing about dinner, but I said that I was too full from tea to think about eating anything soon.

After Rosalie left and my parents went up to the restaurant, I lay on my bed and read for a while. At about eight-thirty I suddenly felt a few hunger pangs. It's funny how stuffing yourself makes you even hungrier later, I thought. I decided to head down to the dining saloon to see if I could get some dinner before it was too late. Just as I walked into the huge room someone called my name. It was Johnnie, waving me over to his table.

"You haven't met my family," he said as he introduced me to his father and older sister Suzette, who was in her twenties. Clearly, Miss Bowen had not ratted us out to Johnnie's dad, as he was quite friendly. But Miss Bowen stared at me coolly from across the table.

I explained that my parents were dining in the Ritz restaurant that evening.

"We'd ask you to join us, Jamie," Mr. Ryerson said, "except we're almost finished. But look," he added, gesturing to a nearby table, "there's Jack Thayer sitting alone. His parents are dining upstairs tonight, too. Here, let me take you over."

Before I had time to protest, Mr. Ryerson had sat me down opposite Jack Thayer, introduced us, and returned to his family. Jack didn't seem thrilled at first about sitting with a kid like me — I soon learned that he was seventeen — but after we chatted a little, he warmed up. He had already had soup and an appetizer so I ordered sirloin of beef to arrive at the same time as his roast duckling.

"I've heard we might see icebergs," I said as we waited for our main courses to arrive.

"Yes, when my mother was sitting on deck today, Mr. Ismay showed her a wireless message from another ship saying there was ice ahead."

"I was in the Marconi room when a message like that one came in," I said.

"You were?" Jack asked. "How did you get *there*?"

"Oh well," I said casually, "I met the Marconi operator earlier in the voyage."

Jack looked at me rather dubiously but I didn't offer any further explanation. He said his family were neighbours of the Ryersons, in a town called Haverford outside Philadelphia. I told him a few stories about Winchester College, which made him laugh. Then he said that he'd been sent to an English boarding school, too. "But my school doesn't seem so bad compared to yours," he added with a smile.

By the time we had finished eating, not many people were left in the room and I got the impression that the stewards were eager to finish cleaning up the tables. Jack and I decided to adjourn to the Palm Room, and maybe have some dessert there. I decided that I liked Jack Thayer. He seemed a very straightforward person and he laughed easily.

As we walked into the Palm Room the Ryersons were just leaving. Johnnie saw us and came over to me. "Sykes is home!" he said quickly before hurrying back to his family.

"Who's Sykes?" Jack asked.

"Oh, just someone we know," I replied, figuring that Jack might think a pet rat was kids' stuff. But I was glad that Johnnie had managed to retrieve him.

There were still many people seated around the small tables in the Palm Room, listening to the orchestra play. Jack and I walked around but couldn't find a free table. Then we spotted a young man sitting alone. He waved us over and offered his hand as we sat down.

"Hello, my name's Milton Long," he said.

Jack and I introduced ourselves and it wasn't long before we were talking about skiing. Milton was from Springfield, Massachusetts, but had recently been skiing in Switzerland. Jack had been to Switzerland, too, so they talked about how wonderful it was to ski there. I was about to ask whether they had ever tried the Laurentians, but then thought that they might not measure up to the Swiss Alps.

"I thought of doing the Cresta Run," Milton said, "but then I remembered that my parents only have one son!" When he saw my puzzled look, Milton explained that the Cresta was a famous but dangerous bobsled run which you are required to go down headfirst.

"But then, of course," he added, "I've never told my parents about being shipwrecked in Alaska, either."

"Shipwrecked?" Jack and I asked in unison.

"Well, it wasn't as exciting as it sounds," he admitted. "I was in a small steamer that ran aground on the rocks. But as it was tipping over I managed to jump onto some shoals and then just went from one rock to another until I got to shore. I only got my feet wet!"

I felt like a real kid as Jack and Milton talked. I'd done so little compared to them. And Milton had been everywhere, it seemed. At one point he asked us to guess his age. I said twenty-two, and Jack guessed twenty-six, but Milton told us he was twenty-nine. That made me feel a little better — he was more than twice my age!

Jack asked Milton if he had collected stamps on his travels — it was a favourite hobby of Jack's. There had been a stamp club at my school, but it had always seemed a really dull pastime to me and I grew a little bored as Jack and Milton talked about stamps. Then Jack noticed his parents coming down the stairs after their dinner. Yikes! I thought, remembering that I was supposed to have stayed in my room all evening! I quickly shook hands with Milton and Jack, thanked them for their company and hurried over to the grand staircase and ran up to B deck. When my parents returned from dinner they found me lying on my bed reading.

"We had such a lovely dinner!" my mother said. "The food was out of this world! And you, dear?"

"Oh, you know, fine, quiet, nothing much," I replied, faking sleepiness. They said good-night and before long the light under their door went out. But I was enjoying *Captains Courageous* and decided to read on until the end of the chapter.

CHAPTER SIX
COLLISION

April 14, 1912, 11:40 p.m.

I had fallen asleep with the book in my hand. Groggily, I sat up and tossed it onto the wooden nightstand beside the bed. Then I turned to switch off the small lamp on the wall. As I did so, its glass shade began to rattle. All of a sudden the whole room swayed — it felt as if we had hit a large wave. And then I heard a long, low, grinding noise. Suddenly I was wide awake. I hopped out of bed and opened the porthole. The ocean below looked perfectly calm and the stars were winking brightly against the ink-black sky. When I climbed back into bed I noticed that the sound of the engines had stopped. It left a strange silence — I had become quite used to their thrumming rhythm. Then I heard voices and footsteps in the corridor outside.

"Something's up," I thought. I put on my slippers and walked across the room to get my overcoat. That's when I noticed light coming from below the door to my parents' room.

"Jamie, is everything all right?" my father called out in a sleepy voice.

"I'm just going up to see why we've stopped," I replied.

"Wait," he said. "I'll come with you."

"No need," I replied. "I'll be fine."

"Wait! I'll be there presently," he insisted, which annoyed me. Surely I was able to go up on deck on my own! My father soon appeared wearing his coat and black bowler hat. He had put on his shoes, but I could see the legs of his flannel pyjamas below his overcoat. All was now quiet in the corridor as we walked aft toward the grand staircase. On the stairs up to A deck we met Mr. Hays and a young man, whom I later learned was his son-in-law. Both were still in their evening clothes and Hays had his ever-present cigar in his hand.

"Good evening, Laidlaw!" he called out. "We've struck an iceberg. But it's gone on by. Nothing to worry about, nothing to worry about at all," he stated firmly. "There's some ice in the water if you want to see it," he added, pointing to the promenade with his cigar.

As we walked onto the A-deck promenade my father said to me quietly, "Hays and his family are guests of Mr. Ismay. So I suppose he knows what he's talking about."

"Have you seen the ice?" asked a grey-bearded man standing by the promenade windows.

When we looked over we realized it was Major Peuchen. He led us forward to the end of the promenade and pointed over the side. We looked down but couldn't see any ice in the water.

"Well, there was some there only moments ago," he said. "I could see it quite clearly."

I went farther aft on the promenade, leaned out and, sure enough, in the black water below lay some greyish chunks of ice.

"Yes, it's there, I can see it!" I said, gesturing to my father and Major Peuchen to come and look.

We heard shouts coming from the lower decks behind us so we walked back and looked over the railing down to the aft well deck. Some young fellows from third class were playing soccer with a chunk of ice. Each time they kicked it, splinters broke off.

"Ow-w, me foot!" I heard an Irish voice yell as one boy hopped about after kicking the ice a little too enthusiastically.

"Pieces from the iceberg fell off as it scraped by us," said Major Peuchen.

"How big was it?" asked my father.

"Must have been a fairly large one," Major Peuchen replied. "Some chaps in the smoking room saw it pass by and thought we'd collided with a sailing ship."

Then he suddenly said, "Hello-o. We seem to be listing! She shouldn't be doing that!" He was holding his arm straight out with his palm downwards. "I think we're listing to starboard!"

My father and I imitated the Major's hand gesture, but neither of us could tell if the ship was leaning to one side or not.

Father turned to me "Well, Jamie," he said, "perhaps we should go down and look in on your mother." We said goodnight to Major Peuchen and returned to the grand staircase.

"Peuchen is a yachtsman," he said as we descended to our deck. "But I doubt he knows much about steamships."

Mother greeted us in her dressing gown when we re-entered our cabin. "The steward was just here, saying something about an iceberg," she reported in a peevish voice. "He says we're to put on our lifebelts and go up on deck. Do you think that's *really* necessary, Henry?"

"Just a precaution, I'm sure," my father replied. "Though we just ran into Peuchen on the deck. He seems to think we're listing to starboard."

"Yes," replied my mother with a slight sniff, "Well, he *would*, wouldn't he."

Suddenly there was a sharp rap at the door. It was a steward, but not our regular one. He had a lifebelt over his arm.

"Everyone is to report to the boat deck," he said brusquely. "Dress warmly and put on your lifebelts. If you need 'elp with 'em, someone will assist you."

My father looked at him coldly, clearly annoyed at being spoken to in this way by a steward. "Is this *really* an emergency?" he demanded. "Or is it simply a drill?"

"Nothin' to worry about, sir," the steward said. "I'm just tellin' you my orders." Then he paused and said, "But from what I've 'eard, this is no drill." With that he left and within seconds we heard him knocking on the door next to ours.

As my father closed the door I noticed for the first time a slight look of worry on his face. A chilly nervous tremor ran down my spine. This was all becoming exciting! I suddenly pictured myself having an even better story to tell the boys at Bishop's College. I pulled out my suitcase from under the bed and began rummaging through it for some warm clothes.

Just then there was another knock on our door and Rosalie entered, wearing her lifebelt over her coat. "There 'as been a collision," she said.

"Yes, with an iceberg," I replied. "But they say it's not serious."

"I'm not so sure. Down below you could really feel it," she said. "And I 'eard from a steward — they are hauling bags out of the mailroom, which is all flooded."

"Yes, Rosalie," my father responded. "But I'm sure that's no cause for alarm. We are to report to the boat deck, but it's likely just a precaution," he concluded in his best take-charge voice.

Rosalie went into my parents' room while I found a warm sweater to wear underneath my overcoat and lifebelt. As I was dressing I thought about what Major Peuchen had said about the *Titanic*'s watertight compartments. Surely they would prevent the ship from sinking. And there were likely other ships nearby that could come to our rescue. But imagine this happening to a brand new ship! What bad luck!

CHAPTER SEVEN
TO THE LIFEBOATS

April 15, 1912, 12:35 p.m.

As we walked toward the grand staircase, I noticed the Fortunes in the corridor ahead of us. Mr. Fortune seemed twice his usual size, as he was wearing a huge, shaggy coat under his lifebelt. At the stairs he turned to let his wife and daughters go up ahead of him and then he spotted us.

"Henry!" he called out to my father. "At last I've found a use for the buffalo coat that everyone has had such fun about!"

"No one can say that Canadians don't know how to dress for the cold!" my father replied as we began to ascend the staircase behind him.

When we stepped through the door onto the boat deck, however, all conversation stopped, because steam was being vented with a deafening roar through pipes that ran up the sides of the funnels. It made me realize just how much steam was required to power the *Titanic*'s engines. Officer Lightoller was shouting out orders beside the portside boat davits, trying to make himself heard above the noise. The canvas covers had been taken off the tops of the lifeboats and one boat had already been swung out over the side. Were they really going to put us all into the lifeboats? I wondered. Looking out on the horizon, I could see the lights of another ship that seemed only a few miles away. Perhaps they were going to row some of the women and children over to it as a precaution?

Suddenly the roar of the steam stopped and Officer Lightoller called out for someone to give him a hand. Major Peuchen stepped forward wearing a lifebelt over his warm overcoat. Trust the Major to be in the middle of things, I thought to myself. He'll be giving orders to Officer Lightoller before long. But the Major did as Lightoller instructed and helped to lift a mast with a sail wrapped around it out of the lifeboat. Then I heard voices from the deck below. Lightoller leaned over the rail to listen to them.

"The windows down 'ere are locked!" a crewman shouted. Lightoller yelled back that he would send someone down to unlock them. He had apparently lowered the first lifeboat down to A deck, thinking it would be easier for passengers to board from there, perhaps forgetting that there were windows on the A-deck promenade.

I heard another forceful voice nearby and turned to see Mr. Hays talking to my father. "I'll take my chances with the big boat," he was saying. "She's good for eight to ten hours at least, and someone will surely have come to our rescue before then. There's a ship out there now," he added, pointing to the lights out beyond the portside railing.

The second lifeboat on the port side was now ready for boarding, but not many women seemed willing to get into it. I couldn't blame them. The deck of the *Titanic* seemed a much safer place than being lowered down into the ocean in that small boat in the middle of the night. Many of the women clung to their husbands.

"Women and children!" Lightoller's voice rang out. "Women and children, please come forward!"

Eventually a few of them were persuaded to step into the boat.

"I don't think Jamie and I need to go yet, do you, Henry?" my mother asked.

"I don't think they want *me* in the boat, Mother," I protested. "I'm not a child!"

"We will follow orders and do as we are told, James!" my father said sternly.

"Any more women?" Lightoller's voice rang out again. "Any more women? Step forward, please!"

All of a sudden we heard a whooshing noise as a white rocket shot into the air and then burst with a loud bang and a cascade of stars.

"They wouldn't be firing rockets if it wasn't serious," one woman said.

The second lifeboat was not full, but Lightoller seemed anxious to launch it. "All right, then," he called out after the rocket noise had stopped. "Lower away!"

Crewmen at either end of the davit began to let out their ropes to lower the lifeboat. It creaked and jerked its way down and then stopped when it was about even with C deck. It looked only half filled. Then the crewman in the stern of the boat called up that he needed another man to help him row.

"I need another seaman in this boat!" Lightoller shouted.

But there was no response. The only two crewmen nearby were needed to help lower the boat.

"Another seaman, please!" Lightoller shouted again.

At that Major Peuchen stepped forward. "I am a yachtsman, if I can be of any use to you, sir," he said to Lightoller.

"If you're enough of a sailor to climb down into that boat, go ahead," Lightoller replied, pointing to the ropes that were holding the lifeboat.

They were hanging about ten feet out from the side of the deck. I wouldn't want to try that, I thought.

"You'd better go below, break a window and climb aboard that way," a voice said. I turned and saw that it was Captain Smith speaking.

"I don't think that would be feasible, sir," Major Peuchen said, shaking his head.

He paused for a moment on the side of the deck. Then he suddenly leapt out and grabbed one of the ropes, quickly wrapping his legs around it.

"Bravo, Arthur!" my father murmured as the Major shinnied about twenty-five feet down into the lifeboat.

"That took courage!" I said aloud, feeling a little guilty for some of my earlier thoughts about the Major.

"Yes," agreed Mr. Molson, who was standing nearby. "And he's not a young man."

A few minutes later a second rocket shot up and exploded in another burst of white stars over the funnels. Surely that ship on the horizon will see that and come over to us, I thought.

When the rocket's noise stopped, the cheery sound of "Alexander's Ragtime Band" could be heard. The ship's orchestra was playing out on the deck beside the gymnasium. The lively tune seemed to lift everyone's spirits. Lightoller was calling out for women to board another lifeboat but, once again, not many were willing to climb aboard.

"I think we can wait a while yet," I heard Mrs. Fortune say to my mother.

I wasn't so sure. The bow of the ship was definitely getting lower in the water. I could feel the forward slant of the deck under my feet. I hoped those watertight compartments were working. But the sound of another ragtime tune made me feel that everything must be all right.

Suddenly I thought of Johnnie and realized that I hadn't seen him or his family on the boat deck. Could they already have left in a lifeboat? I decided to have a look over on the starboard side. Telling my mother and father that I was just going into the gymnasium to warm up for a minute, I quickly scurried across the deck.

Two officers were supervising the lowering of a boat when I got to the starboard side. There were a number of men in the boat, not just women and children. I assumed that the officers on this side of the ship hadn't been as strict as Lightoller about not allowing men in the boats. Then I saw Mr. Hays standing beside the davit, waving to Mrs. Hays and their daughter in the lifeboat. His son-in-law was beside him. Mr. Hays must believe it's safe to stay on the *Titanic*, I thought, since he could have gone in that boat.

I walked farther aft along the starboard side but didn't see any sign of Johnnie, so I decided I'd better rejoin my parents before they got worried about me. As I turned, I spotted Jack and Milton standing beside the railing near the third funnel. I waved to get their attention but they didn't see me, so I hurried back to my parents. When I returned to the port side, another lifeboat was being loaded. Captain Smith was there with a megaphone in his hand. "Any more ladies?" he shouted through it. "Any more ladies?"

An elderly couple approached the boat. The husband helped his wife into the boat and then started to climb in himself.

"No men allowed, sir! Women and children only!" Lightoller called out.

"I'm sure no one would object if this gentleman accompanied his wife," I heard someone say.

"Women and children only! Those are my orders!" Lightoller said firmly.

The woman stood up in the boat and gestured to be helped out. Several men stepped forward to lift her back onto the deck. She took her husband by the arm. "We've been together too long for me to leave you now," I heard her say to him. "Where you go, I go." They walked away slowly down the deck, arm in arm.

Captain Smith was giving orders to the crewman in the stern of the lifeboat. "Row across to that ship," he said, pointing to the lights on the horizon. "Land your passengers and then come back for more."

The crewmen began letting out the ropes to lower the boat. I felt my mother shiver next to me and suggested that we go into the gymnasium to warm up.

Father and Rosalie came with us. Inside, a few people were sitting on the exercise machines. Was it only two days ago that the red-faced gym instructor had thrown Johnnie and me out of there?

We could still hear the musicians playing outside the gym's windows. After about five minutes we went back out onto the deck, and as we did a man in a bowler hat came out of the first-class entrance. I realized that it was Mr. Andrews, the Irishman who had shown us the rooms in third class on sailing day. He walked right over to me, put his arm on my shoulder and led me away from the musicians.

"The ladies *must* get into a lifeboat as soon as possible," he said. "There is very little time to wait.

Please do as I say." Then he immediately left us and approached another group of passengers with the same message.

"Who *is* that man?" my mother asked in a startled voice.

"That's Mr. Andrews!" I blurted out. "He's the man who designed the ship. He knows what he's talking about!"

For the first time I saw a really worried look cross my father's face. The slant of the deck was now very noticeable.

We hurried over to the lifeboat that Officer Lightoller was loading. It was filling up more quickly than any of the previous ones. Charles Fortune was helping one of his sisters into it. His mother and her maid and two other sisters were already seated in the boat. When they saw us they gestured to my mother that there was room beside them. Father immediately helped Rosalie into the boat and then turned to my mother. But I had already taken her hand and was guiding her into the boat.

She sat down beside Mrs. Fortune and then called out to me. "Jamie, you come too! You *must* come!"

"No boys!" Officer Lightoller's voice rang out loudly, and I felt my face turn crimson.

"Don't worry, I'll be fine!" I called to her as

the boat began to make its descent. "I'll look after Father," I added. "We'll see you on the boat to New York!"

I waved and she looked back at us unhappily, but Rosalie gave me a smile and a wave.

While the boat was being lowered, I suddenly heard a few cries from the women in it. A small man had jumped into the boat from A deck. Some of the women were speaking harshly to him but he wriggled onto a seat and hunkered down. My father shook his head disapprovingly.

Crowds of people were now milling about on the deck and the mood was becoming a little more urgent. Three boats were being loaded on the port side. I saw a steward lead a group of women and children from third class toward the one nearest me. I remembered climbing up from the third-class quarters with Frank Browne and Jack Odell on the first day. It would have been difficult for people to find their way from down there all the way up to the boat deck.

Suddenly I spotted Johnnie and his family walking toward us in a crowd of people.

"Johnnie!" I shouted out and waved at him.

He hurried right over. "We've been waiting one deck down for about an hour for *that* boat there," he said, pointing to the davit holding the first lifeboat that had been put over the side. "But nobody's been able to get into it."

We suddenly heard a commotion on the deck and turned to look. A crowd of men was shoving their way toward one of the boats. An officer beside the boat shouted and raised his hand. I was astounded to see a revolver in it. Had the crowd got *that* desperate? He pointed the pistol straight up and fired two shots into the air. The crowd shrunk back.

"Looks like the rats want to leave the sinking ship," Johnnie said. "Speaking of rats," he added casually, "I went back to my room and let Sykes out of his cage."

"I've been thinking about Max," I said. "He might be trapped in the kennel. He won't stand a chance if the boat sinks — "

"*When* the boat sinks, you mean," replied Johnnie. "Hey, let's go and let the dogs out! Somebody has to do it!"

I knew my father would never allow it, so I hurried over to him and said I was just going back into the gymnasium to warm up for a minute. He nodded. Then Johnnie and I began walking up the slanting deck.

"Please return to A deck!" a voice shouted. "We will be loading your lifeboat from A deck!"

We'd made it some way along the deck when suddenly Johnnie's sister was beside us, taking Johnnie by the arm. "We have to go back down one deck, John!" Suzette said. "You must come *now!* Mother panicked when she saw you were gone."

"But we have to let the dogs out — "

"The dogs! There isn't time! And *you* had better come too," Suzette snapped at me.

"But my dog is in the kennels — " I started to say.

"Someone will take care of the dogs!" she insisted. "You both have to come *now!*"

"Come with us, Jamie!" Johnnie said. "There might be room for all of us."

The slant of the deck was growing ever steeper. When I looked aft I could see that the deck near the stern was now higher than where we were standing. I hurried back to my father, who was talking with Mr. Molson.

"There you are!" my father said, "I was starting to get worried."

"We've been told to go down one deck," I said. "At least it will be warmer there."

"All right," he agreed. He turned and shook Mr. Molson's hand and came with me.

"Looks like this will be the millionaire's lifeboat," my father commented as we walked down the staircase behind the Ryersons, the Astors and other rich-looking Americans. Many of the women were wearing fur coats over their nightgowns. When we arrived on the A-deck promenade I saw that several deck chairs had been placed below the open windows to act as ramps into the lifeboat. Officer Lightoller jumped up and placed one foot on the gunwale of the lifeboat and another on a windowsill. Perspiration beaded his face in spite of the cold air. He had taken off his officer's jacket and was wearing only a blue seaman's sweater and trousers. I could see his pyjamas showing below his trouser cuffs.

"Come along now," he called out, "the boat is quite safe!"

Mr. Astor came forward with his young, pregnant wife on his arm. She was obviously very anxious and he was trying to reassure her in a low, soothing voice. He helped her up the deck-chair ramp and across the windowsill into the boat, then turned to Lightoller and asked, "May I accompany my wife? She is in a delicate condition."

"No sir," Lightoller replied. "No men are allowed in these boats until the women are loaded first."

"What boat is this?" Astor asked.

"Number Four," Lightoller said.

Then Johnnie's family came forward. Mr. Ryerson

suddenly noticed that Victorine was not wearing a lifebelt. He took his off and put it on her, then helped her and his two daughters and Miss Bowen up the ramp and into the boat. Finally he embraced his wife, who kept a firm grip on Johnnie's hand as they went up to the windowsill together.

"That boy can't go!" Lightoller insisted.

"Of course that boy goes with his mother — he's only thirteen!" Mr. Ryerson shouted indignantly at Lightoller. He then pushed Johnnie through the open window after his mother.

Lightoller grimaced and called out. "All right. But no more boys!"

Farther back in the line, I saw a woman standing with her daughter and a son who looked to be about eight. The mother took off her large hat and put it on her son's head. All three of them climbed into Lifeboat Four with no protests from Lightoller.

"How many women are in that boat?" a voice called down from the boat deck above us.

"Twenty-four," someone answered.

"That's enough," came the response. "Lower away!"

"How many seamen have you?" another voice asked.

"One," came the reply.

A second seaman quickly shinnied down a

rope and into the boat just before it began to be lowered.

I was standing near an open window and saw Mr. Astor blow a kiss to his wife and then toss her his gloves. I tried to wave to Johnnie, but he was hunched down in the boat with his head lowered. The boat reached the water very quickly — it was now only about fifteen feet below us. I thought again about Max being trapped in his cage in the kennel.

"What about the dogs?" I asked, turning to Mr. Astor. "What will happen to them?"

"I spoke to a crewman earlier," Mr. Astor replied. "He told me he'd go back to the kennel and let all the dogs out of their cages."

I felt a little better after he said that. At least Max stood a chance now.

Officer Lightoller hurried by us and opened a door marked *For Use of Crew Only*. Mr. Astor and several other men followed him. I waved to my father that we should do the same. It was an iron staircase, so narrow that we had to brace ourselves to climb up it, since the ship was now listing toward the port side. When I looked down and saw water lapping up the steps only a few decks below us, I was shocked. The stairway lamps were shining through the water like lights in a swimming pool.

Thumps and rumbling and the sounds of china breaking rose up from below. I clasped the metal railing and climbed upward one step at a time. When I glanced at my watch I saw that it was a few minutes before two a.m. It occurred to me that I'd never been up this late before.

CHAPTER EIGHT

The Final Minutes

April 15, 1912, 2:00 a.m.

On the boat deck I waited for my father to come up the stairs behind me. Overhead, the sky was a mass of stars. The forecastle deck where Johnnie and I had stood on the windlass was now completely awash, the foremast surrounded by water. But the light above the crow's nest was still shining red. At the stern, many people were milling about and more third-class passengers continued to stream up on deck from below. Barrels and deck chairs — anything that would float — were being thrown over the side by men preparing to jump. I saw Thomas Andrews pick up a deck chair and heave it into the water. Another man was shinnying down the rope from an empty davit arm into the water.

"They're loading *that* boat," my father said, grabbing my arm and pointing forward.

Lightoller and some other crewmen had fitted another boat into a pair of empty davits.

"It's a collapsible boat, with canvas sides," I heard a man say as we joined the group standing near it.

"Women and children only!" Officer Lightoller called out when the boat was ready.

Third-class women in coats and shawls were escorted forward, some of them carrying children.

"Any more women?" Lightoller shouted when the boat was about half full.

"There *are* no more women!" a voice in the crowd yelled as several men clambered into the boat.

"Out *now*, all of you!" ordered Lightoller as he pulled one man out. The others sheepishly followed.

"Link arms and form a ring!" Lightoller called to the crewmen near him. I walked forward and linked arms with one of them. A moment later my father took my other arm. I looked up at him and he gave me a nod and a small, tense smile. Soon others joined us in the line. An American man came up to us with his wife, who had her arm in a sling. She was allowed through and was helped into the boat. Her husband was told he couldn't go any farther.

"Yes, I know," he said sadly. "I will stay."

Another man rushed up with two toddlers in his arms and handed them over to be put into the boat.

"*Mes fils* — my little boys," he said in a strong French accent. "My name is Hoffman."

A woman in the boat made room for the two boys beside her. The boat now looked fairly full and no more women were coming forward.

"Lower away!" Lightoller ordered and the boat creaked down the side.

"That's the last boat, boys!" I heard one of the men in the crowd say. "Every man for himself now!"

My father turned toward me. He was perspiring heavily and his breath was coming in short bursts. I had never seen him look this way before.

"Jamie, you're a good swimmer," he said. "I remember you diving into those waves at St. Andrews — "

"Father." I grabbed his arm. "We're going to make it. *Both* of us — "

"Yes, yes," he said. "Of course we will. But just in case . . . you need to know . . . I've provided for your mother and you . . . Arthur will see to things . . . I love you, my son." He gripped my shoulder. "Tell your mother I love her, too."

His eyes were full of tears. My father was not a man who expressed his emotions easily. He had never, *ever* spoken to me like this before. I didn't know what to say. Finally, he recovered and cleared his throat. "Perhaps we should head toward the stern," he said more calmly.

Suddenly a noise from above made us all look up. Some men were clambering onto the roof of the officers' cabins behind the bridge. I could see that at least one more collapsible lifeboat had been stored there.

"We should help!" I said to my father. "That boat could be our last chance! I can get up there if you can boost me."

"What a stupid place to put a lifeboat," he said, but I was already running over toward it.

I clasped the top of the cabin window frame and tried to clamber upwards, but soon lost my grip and fell back to the deck. I needed to get out of my bulky lifebelt and long overcoat so I began stripping them off.

"I'll boost you up, Jamie," my father said, "but you *must* wear your lifebelt."

I threw my coat to the deck and quickly tied on the lifebelt over my sweater. My father cupped his hands for my foot and then hoisted me onto his shoulders. Through a lighted window I could see into an officer's cabin, with its single bed and desk. The ship suddenly lurched, causing my father to stagger a little, but I was able to grasp the railing overhead. I pulled myself onto the roof and grabbed onto one of the thick mooring cables that ran from the deck up to the huge funnel above me.

Officer Lightoller was leaning over one end of the collapsible lifeboat, hacking away at the ropes that held it to the deck. "Out of the way, son!" he called out sharply when I came near. He cut away furiously at the last of the ropes and then looked up at me again. I suddenly wondered if he recognized me as one of the boys he had marched off the forecastle deck a few days ago. It seemed completely unimportant now.

"We have to somehow shift 'er down to the deck!" Lightoller said, breathing heavily. "See if you can organize some planks."

I ran over to the edge of the roof and called down to my father that we needed some boards to help slide the boat downwards. Then I clambered down the sloping roof to the other end of the boat. "It looks awfully small," I said to a crewman who was standing astride it to balance himself.

"Bigger with the sides up," he replied, "Could hold maybe sixty of us — *if* we can launch it."

From this end of the roof I could look down on the *Titanic*'s bow. The forecastle and well decks were submerged now, with only the tip of the bow railing still above water. I turned to look toward the stern. It occurred to me that the propellers must be lifting out of the water, and I shivered — from the cold or fear or both. My heart was thumping hard against the wall of my chest. On the slanting deck near the stern, people were buzzing about like insects — hundreds of them. Passengers from the lower decks were still pouring out through the stairway doors. Had they been down below all this time? I peered toward the horizon, hoping that the ship's light we'd seen earlier was still there. I couldn't see it.

Shouts erupted from the starboard side of the roof. Some crewmen had managed to free another collapsible boat that was stowed there. Then my father's voice came up from the deck below. He and some others were leaning oars against the wall of the officer's quarters to act as a ramp to the boat deck. I hoped they would be sturdy enough to do the job.

A man near the stern of our collapsible boat called out, "All right lads, let's all give 'er a go."

I joined the others in pushing the stern end of the lifeboat toward the edge of the roof. Then we ran up to the bow and pushed it as well.

"Stand clear below!" Lightoller shouted as we nudged the boat to the edge of the roof. Just then the *Titanic* lurched, causing the lifeboat to slide off the roof and crash down to the deck below. The oars splintered beneath it. I rushed over to make sure my father hadn't been hurt. I couldn't see him at first, but then caught sight of him being pulled backwards within a crowd of men who were charging up the sloping deck. He looked up toward me and touched his forehead in a kind of salute. Then he was swallowed up by the crowd.

With a gurgling roar a huge wave rolled toward me from the bow of the ship. It washed right below the roof where I stood, heading for the crowds retreating up the deck. Some people fell back and were engulfed. I looked for my father but couldn't see him. The lifeboat we had been trying to launch washed off upside down. Then the ship lurched downwards again.

She's going under! I thought. I'll be sucked down with her!

I slid down to the forward end of the roof. A wall of greenish water was surging toward me. I thought of the surf crashing onto the beach at St. Andrews. I knew what I had to do — it was my only chance.

I dived right into the wave.

The freezing water nearly knocked me out. It was like being pierced by thousands of needles. I felt myself being dragged down so I kicked upward. Gasping, I came to the surface. Ahead stood the foremast with the crow's nest almost level with me. My first thought was to swim toward it. Then I realized I had to get clear of the ship! At that instant I was violently sucked back and slammed against something hard. I could feel some wire grating and realized I was trapped over an air shaft, with the sea pouring down into it. I prayed the grating would hold.

If this is the end, I thought, let it be quick. Then a blast of hot air came rushing up the shaft and blew me free. Coughing, spluttering, I bobbed to the surface, gasping for air. I had to get away from the ship! I began paddling away as quickly as I could.

Ropes, deck chairs and pieces of wood swirled by me. I could just make out the shapes of other swimmers. I ducked as a barrel nearly hit me. Then I heard shouts as the huge forward funnel came crashing down in a blaze of sparks. It caused a wave that pushed me farther away from the sinking ship. I saw the *Titanic* standing at a slant against the starry sky, with all her lights still shining. Crowds of people were clinging to the stern. Others were falling, tumbling down into the sea.

I pushed aside some debris and swam on.

My lifebelt kept me afloat, but it was hard to

swim with it. I splashed forward, desperate to find a lifeboat or something to clamber onto. My feet and hands were numb. I wanted to rest but I knew I had to keep moving. Then my arm bumped against something hard and I grasped it. This was too big to be debris, I thought. Reaching up, I realized it was an overturned lifeboat. A hand reached down and pulled me up, and I crawled onto the lifeboat's back.

"Steady now! One slip and you'll tip us," a voice said. I recognized it as Officer Lightoller's. I could see traces of his breath in the freezing air, and make out the shapes of other men trying to balance along the keel of the overturned boat.

"Thank you," I said through chattering teeth. It took me a few minutes to catch my breath. Then I stood up and looked back. The stern of the *Titanic* was now high in the air. Incredibly, her lights were still glowing. Then they blinked once and went out.

Suddenly I heard what sounded like explosions. In the darkness, sparks began shooting up from the middle of the ship. Then she broke in two. The forward part of the *Titanic* slid under the black water and the severed stern settled back. Then it, too, slowly filled with water. Screams came from those clinging to it as it sank. Soon all I could see was the sky filled with a mass of stars. All around me were howling voices.

"Father!" I yelled at the top of my lungs. "Father!" But the wailing din drowned out my call. After a while the noise died down a little, so I shouted once again, but there was no reply.

"Jamie?" a voice near me called out.

I leaned toward it. "Jack!" I answered. "Jack Thayer?"

"Yes, it's me," he replied in a low voice.

"Are you all right?" I asked.

"Yes," he said with a shiver. "But so cold."

I thought back to our dinner in the dining saloon — could it really have been only a few hours ago? Both of us listening to Milton Long in the Palm Room as he told us of his adventures in Alaska. It seemed unbelievable that everything in that huge room now lay at the bottom of the ocean.

From the stern end of the boat I heard splashing sounds. Some of the men were trying to paddle with pieces of wood they had picked up, and one or two had oars. Some swimmers were coming near, desperate to get onto our boat, but there were cries of, "No, no, one more would sink us!"

I felt incredibly lucky to have been allowed on board.

I watched one man swim up beside us, only

to be told how overloaded we were. "That's all right boys, keep cool," he replied calmly. As he swam off, he called back, "Good luck, boys. God bless you."

The awful sound of wailing voices continued. As we got farther away it became an eerie, high-pitched drone that went on and on and then slowly began to die down.

I suddenly thought of my father. "I hope my father got pulled into a boat," I said to Jack.

"Mine too," he replied. "And Milton. We were together by the rail. He jumped first. But he told me he couldn't swim very well."

Before long the last of the wailing voices stopped. Soon all was quiet on the calm sea.

From the stern of our boat, a voice asked, "Don't you think we ought to pray?"

There was a murmur of agreement. Then, in a deep, clear voice came the words, "Our Father, who art in heaven, hallowed be thy name . . . "

CHAPTER NINE
ON AN OVERTURNED BOAT

April 15, 1912, 3:00 a.m.

"Boat ahoy!" we shouted in unison. "Boat ahoy!"

We waited, but in return there was only silence. A few men kept on yelling hoarsely, until they grew tired and stopped. It was intensely cold. My hair was stuck to my forehead. My legs felt rubbery from standing and I longed to sit down. But any sudden movement could capsize our overturned boat. With every motion, the air was leaking from underneath it and we were slowly sinking lower in the water.

"How many are we?" asked Officer Lightoller. From farther back there came only mumbles and a few groans. Lightoller repeated the question in a commanding voice but no one responded.

"We will obey what the officer orders!" a crewman with a Cockney accent suddenly shouted from the stern. Lightoller then asked that all men present say "aye," one after the other. We did so and he counted twenty-eight ayes. Twenty-eight men on the back of this one small boat, I thought. Could it hold us all up until rescue arrived? And *would* rescue arrive?

"Harold Bride, the Marconi fellow, is back 'ere," another voice answered. "Maybe he knows what boats are near us."

"What ships answered the distress call, Bride?" Lightoller shouted.

"The *Baltic* and the *Olympic*," said an exhausted voice, which I recognized as that of the younger wireless operator. "But the *Carpathia* was the nearest. Said she was coming fast."

This gave us all some hope.

Then we saw some green flares on the horizon. Were these from a rescue ship or just from one of the lifeboats? The men with boards and oars tried to paddle us in the direction of the flares, but they stopped when the lights disappeared. There were also many shooting stars in the sky, which looked like white rockets. Through chattering teeth we tried to talk to help take our minds off the cold.

"Maybe we'll have a hot breakfast on the *Carpathia*," I said to Jack.

"I'd be happy with a warm blanket," he replied.

Someone wondered what had happened to the ship that we had all clearly seen while the *Titanic* was sinking.

"That ship could only have been five miles away!" one man said.

"Must've been a sailing ship," said another. "A steamer would've come over to help us."

After an hour or so I noticed the sky beginning to lighten. At the same time a breeze began to stir up some small waves that rocked our precarious craft even more.

"Form up into a column!" Lightoller shouted.

The boat shook as some of the men crouching in the stern stood up. Lightoller organized us into a double line standing along the keel facing forward, holding on to each other by the shoulders. Jack and I were near the bow just behind Lightoller. All of us followed his orders each time he called, "Lean to the left! . . . Stand upright! . . . Lean right!" as we tried to counteract the waves. The movement made me feel a little warmer, even though our feet were only inches above the water.

As dawn began to lighten the sky, I saw Venus, the morning star, still shining after all the others had vanished. On the horizon a faint crescent moon appeared.

Then came a splash. One man had slipped overboard. Several of us made to reach for him, but Lightoller shouted, "*Stop!* No one move!"

"He's dead!" someone shouted. We all knew

there was no point in risking our own lives to retrieve a corpse.

The ominous splashes would happen twice more. Each time it was horrible. Each time I caught myself feeling relieved, knowing that it lightened the load on our boat. I later felt ashamed, and sorry for the men who had died from the cold and exposure. Suddenly there was a shout from the stern. "There's a steamer coming up behind us!"

"Stand steady!" commanded Lightoller. "I will be the one to look astern!"

We all stood still while Lightoller turned to look, but he did not confirm the good news. Soon, however, we could see lights in the distance that were unmistakeably the mast lights of a steamer. Behind her were large white shapes that some of us thought might be sailing ships. One man suggested they could be fishing boats from the Grand Banks off Newfoundland. But as the sun rose we saw that they were icebergs, towering and majestic. A double-peaked one had to be at least two hundred feet high. Could one of those be the iceberg that sank us? I wondered. As the sky turned pink, these mountains of ice began to glow in mauve and coral colours.

With the dawn came a stronger breeze that sent waves washing over our boat. Each one rocked the boat and let more air escape from underneath it. The hull became even more slippery and I clasped Jack's shoulders tightly, knowing that one slip would mean certain death.

The lights of the steamer soon disappeared. New fears suddenly sprang into my exhausted brain. Would our boat sink under us before we could be rescued? Would the steamer miss us altogether? Maybe it would run right over us!

When the sun came up fully we could see the steamer about four or five miles away. Some of the *Titanic*'s lifeboats were rowing toward her. But could we last long enough for her to get to us? Our feet were now soaked and freezing from the waves washing over them.

"Boat off the starboard bow!" called one of the crewmen near the stern.

I kept my body steady but turned my head. Four of the *Titanic*'s lifeboats were tied together in a line about 800 yards away.

"Boat ahoy!" we yelled at the top of our lungs. "Boat ahoy!"

The lifeboats didn't seem to hear us, so Lightoller fished an officer's whistle out of his pocket and blew a shrill blast. We watched as two of the boats untied from the others and began to inch toward us.

"Come over and take us off!" shouted Lightoller when they came within hailing distance.

"Aye, aye, sir," came the reply. The two boats slowly began to draw near. We were so low in the water that the wash as one of the boats came alongside almost tipped us over.

"Steady now, men," Lightoller ordered. "No scrambling or you'll sink us!" He began unloading our boat one man at a time.

Yet each time someone leaned forward to jump into the lifeboat, our boat swayed sickeningly. Jack and I were among the last to go. When my turn finally came I jumped and landed on the floor of the lifeboat near the bow. A woman threw a steamer rug over me. A crewman passed me a flask of whisky and I took a slug. It burned all the way down but helped warm me up. I realized it was the first time I'd ever drunk alcohol.

One man who was in the water paddled over to the lifeboat and was pulled on board. "That's Joughin, the baker," a crewman said. "He's got enough liquor in 'im to keep 'imself good and warm."

Lightoller was the last man to leave the over-turned boat. But first he lifted a body that was lying along the keel and pushed it into the lifeboat. An American passenger who had been with us during the night tried rubbing the lifeless man's face and wrists, but soon realized he was dead. Lightoller then scrambled aboard the lifeboat near me, and quickly made his way to the stern to take control of the tiller.

I put the steamer rug up to my mouth and breathed through it, hoping the warmth would begin to thaw my face.

Suddenly water splashed over the side onto the blanket. The lifeboat was now so overloaded that waves were beginning to wash over its gunwales.

"Some of you in the front," Lightoller shouted, "move back here!"

Jack and I and a few others crawled through the other passengers to the stern of the lifeboat. This helped a little, but we were still dangerously low in the water. We were also moving very slowly since the boat was so difficult to row. I looked up at Lightoller standing by the tiller. His lips were blue from the cold. A woman nearby took off her cape and passed it to him. He shook his head, but she stood up and draped it around his shoulders and then put its hood over his head. He looked slightly odd, but it did seem to warm him a little.

I looked back to the lifeboat being towed behind us. I realized that it was Lifeboat Four, with the Ryersons and Jack's mother on board. I saw Johnnie with his back to me, rowing with one of his sisters. Lightoller soon cut their boat free and they pulled ahead of us. I could see some of the *Titanic*'s other lifeboats drawing near to the ship I assumed was the *Carpathia*. One of them had hoisted a sail and was towing another boat behind it. Soon we were the last of the boats left on the open sea — a sea that was becoming increasingly choppy. Water continued to splash over the sides, making us sink even lower in the water. I wondered how much longer we could last.

Slowly we lumbered ever closer to the waiting rescue ship. We managed to ride out several long swells and some waves that crashed into the boat. Then we coasted on one long wave that took us right into calmer waters in the lee of the *Carpathia*. Light shone from an open gangway door on the side of the ship and a rope ladder hung down from it. It was the most welcoming sight I had ever seen.

Faces appeared over the side of the upper decks and a bo'sun's chair, a kind of sling, was lowered. Officer Lightoller began bundling women onto the chair as quickly as he could. Some of them screamed as they were hoisted up the side. Finally, only the men were left. Most of us managed to scramble up the rope ladder onto the *Carpathia*. As I reached up to grab the bottom rung of the ladder, my lifebelt felt so sodden and heavy I stripped it off and threw it into the sea.

Harold Bride, who was just ahead of me, had feet so badly frostbitten that he sprawled face first onto the deck. I managed to pull myself up and wobble forward. Then I spotted my mother huddled with a group of women.

"Jamie!" she cried, rushing toward me. "Jamie, thank God you're safe. Where's your father?"

"I don't know, Mother," I replied.

Then my knees buckled and everything went black.

CHAPTER TEN
ON THE *CARPATHIA*

April 15, 1912, 8:40 a.m.

Coughing hoarsely, I opened my eyes. My throat was still burning from the whisky I'd drunk in the lifeboat.

"You fainted," said a woman kneeling beside me. She had wrapped a blanket around my shoulders.

Then I heard my mother's voice. "But where are the other boats?" she was asking plaintively. "There must be more boats!"

I struggled to my feet and went over to her. Rosalie was standing beside her in a small group of women. A uniformed man was gently explaining to them that there were no more lifeboats from the *Titanic*.

"But this cannot be!" said a woman with a French accent.

"Could they have climbed onto the icebergs?" asked another woman. "Should you not look there, Captain?"

"What about *that* boat there?" asked my mother,

pointing to a small steamer that had appeared beside us.

"That is the *Californian*," said the captain. "She has only just arrived. They have picked up no one."

"Then . . . we are all widows?" asked the French woman.

"We will have a last look round the area as we depart," the captain replied quietly. Then he headed up to the bridge.

"Come inside," said Rosalie gently to my mother. "Come and have something warm." But my mother clung to the railing, staring out to sea.

"Margaret, let's go inside, shall we?" said a male voice. When the man put his arm around my mother's shoulder, I realized it was Major Peuchen. Mother only stared at him, but allowed him to escort us to the dining saloon.

Inside, it was eerily quiet. People wrapped in blankets were sipping coffee or hot broth. No one was talking. One woman was sobbing quietly into her handkerchief, but everyone else just seemed stunned. I heard the rumble of the ship's engines starting up.

"Broth?" asked a steward carrying a tray of steaming bowls. I nodded and then spooned it up hungrily until a wave of nausea washed over me.

"Jamie, you're looking green!" Rosalie whispered.

Major Peuchen quickly steered me to a toilet, where I vomited up sea water, brandy and beef broth until my sides ached.

"I'll take you to the infirmary," he said when I came out.

"No, no, I'm fine," I insisted. "I just need to lie down for a while."

When we came back to the table, my mother was sitting with Mrs. Fortune. She said little, but did tell me that two rooms had been offered to the Fortunes and that she had been invited to join them. I wondered if there was news about Charles and his father, but thought it better not to ask.

"Jamie," said a voice. I turned to see Jack Thayer standing with one of the *Carpathia*'s passengers. "This lady has kindly offered me the use of her room," he said. "Why don't you come too?"

I looked at my mother and she nodded her approval. I glanced at Rosalie and she waved me off, saying, "I'll be fine. You go."

"How's your mother?" I asked Jack as we walked out of the dining saloon.

"Not too bad, considering," he replied. "Worried about my father, of course. She's in the captain's cabin with two other women."

We followed the *Carpathia* passenger to her room, which turned out to be quite small, with only one bed. I insisted that Jack take it and made a bed for myself on the floor with a few pillows and a quilt. Our clothes were still damp and smelled of sea water. We both stripped to our underpants and passed our clothes out the door to the woman whose cabin we were using. "I'll see if I can have these laundered," I heard her say from the corridor.

"That's most kind of you," replied Jack with his head half out the door.

We tried to wash up as best we could using the small sink.

"Whew," said Jack, pointing to my lower back. "That's a real beauty of a bruise."

I had to turn and look in the mirror to see a large reddish area with purple in the centre. I gave it a poke and winced.

"Well, it looks worse than it is," I replied. I told him about being slammed against the wire grating. "Looks like something got you too," I said, indicating a long red scratch on his neck.

"Yeah, a jagged piece of wood stabbed me just after I hit the water. Still, it's not much, considering."

"Yes, considering," I replied. We both fell silent for a moment.

Exhausted, I sank onto my makeshift bed on the floor. The scent and feel of a fresh pillowcase on my cheek was intoxicating and I instantly fell into a deep sleep.

* * *

The rhythmic sound of the *Carpathia*'s engines woke me gently. When I opened my eyes I wondered what I was doing on the floor. Then I remembered.

Jack's bed was empty and my clothes were lying on it. As I crawled out of bed I felt a stab in my lower back. I checked in the small mirror. The purple patch on my back had grown larger. When I picked up my clothes from the bed they were dry but still unwashed and a little stiff from the salt water. I had no idea what time it was, but I was very hungry. My watch had stopped at 2:15. I realized that must have been the time I had dived into the ocean from the *Titanic*.

"You're up," said Jack, startling me a little as he entered the room.

"Yes. What time is it?"

"Almost two in the afternoon," he replied. "But you can still get some lunch if you hurry. There was a lineup earlier."

I pulled my sweater over my head and we walked down the corridor together. It was hard to believe that it was less than twelve hours since the *Titanic* had sunk — it seemed like days ago.

The *Carpathia*'s small dining saloon was crowded and the stewards seemed a little frazzled with all the extra passengers they had to serve. As Jack and I sat down at a table I saw Johnnie leaving with one of his sisters. I waved to him, but he looked away the moment he spotted me.

"Feeling better?" said a man's voice. It was Major Peuchen. He sat down and began filling us in on all that had happened while we'd slept. He was as talkative as ever.

"Captain Rostron raced through the night at full speed, dodging icebergs, to come to our rescue," he said. "I trust he receives commendation for it."

The Major described how the captain had organized a memorial service in the dining saloon as the *Carpathia* steamed over the site where the *Titanic* had gone down. A *Carpathia* passenger who was a minister had read prayers for both the living and the dead. I was glad that my mother hadn't been there — I knew it would have been too much for her. Major Peuchen had gone out on deck during the service to look at the wreck site, but said that he had seen only floating debris — deck chairs, pieces of wood, lifebelts — and just one body.

"So . . . maybe more people were rescued then?" I asked.

"No, son. I'm sorry. I'm told there's no chance of that," he replied with a sigh. "I believe there are just over seven hundred of us from *Titanic* on board. That means that more than fifteen hundred have . . . have . . . perished." His voice broke. "It's . . . just . . . overwhelming . . . "

The Major, for once, had to stop speaking. I looked at Jack and saw tears in his eyes. My eyes were burning too. Both of us had been hoping that our fathers had somehow survived.

"So . . . there's no hope . . . at all?" I asked.

The Major shook his head with his eyes closed. There was a long silence. Jack put his elbow up over his face and I saw his shoulders heaving. I buried my face in my hands. My heart was thudding as the news sunk in. But no tears came.

"I feel simply terrible about Harry Molson," the Major continued in a halting voice. "He was going to take another ship . . . but I persuaded him . . . to sail with me on the *Titanic*. . . And then there's Mark Fortune and his son . . . both gone . . . And Mrs. Hays and her daughter have lost their husbands . . . young Vivian Payne, too . . . So, so many . . . "

The Major couldn't continue. He pulled out his handkerchief and wiped his eyes. I think he was embarrassed about losing his composure in public. We sat in silence for a few minutes.

"Do you know, I saw the oddest thing," he eventually continued, trying to speak in a more normal voice. "When we passed by where she sank, there was a striped barber's pole floating in the water. The barbershop was on C deck, so that pole must have been blown right out of the ship by one of the explosions we heard."

"Perhaps when the ship broke in two . . . " Jack started to say.

"Oh but she didn't!" the Major interrupted. "She sank in one piece. I'm certain of that."

Jack and I locked eyes. I raised my eyebrows. We both knew what we had seen.

After lunch we discovered that it wasn't possible to walk very far on the crowded decks of the *Carpathia*. *Titanic* passengers sat huddled in groups everywhere and most of the lifeboats had been hoisted on board as well. I counted six of them stowed on the forward deck and saw that others had been put in the *Carpathia*'s davits. It was strange to think that these few boats were all that was left of the huge liner.

Around four that afternoon, the *Carpathia*'s engines suddenly stopped. It had turned windy and chilly by then and most people had gone below, but Jack and I were still out on deck. We saw the captain walking toward the railing with a man in a minister's collar. Behind them came some of the *Carpathia*'s crewmen, carrying four canvas bags. It took me a moment to realize there must be bodies sewn into those bags. We watched with heads bowed as the minister read from his prayer book. "In the midst of life, we are in death," he said. As each canvas bag was brought forward, the minister then read out: "Unto Almighty God we commend the soul of our brother departed, and we commit his body to the deep . . . "

After each body went over the side, we heard a sad, and very final, splash. When the burial service was finished I looked at Jack and knew that it wasn't just the wind that was making his eyes water. We were both thinking of our fathers, wondering if they would ever have a proper burial. We stood together at the railing looking out over the grey sea, wondering if our fathers were floating on it somewhere.

"My father taught me how to handle a sailboat," Jack began to say, but couldn't continue. I laid my arm across his shoulders as he put his forehead down on the railing and wept.

I tried to think back for a similar memory. When I was small my father always seemed older than other boys' fathers. Then I remembered being knocked over by a wave at St. Andrews when I was about four.

My father had raced into the surf and carried me onto the beach and wrapped me in a towel. I remembered how he had called me "little man" as he rubbed me dry. Tears began pouring down my cheeks. I put my hands over my eyes, but hot tears trickled through them. Then I heard myself sobbing aloud. After a few minutes I stopped and pulled out my handkerchief and wiped my face. I suddenly thought about Johnnie, who had now lost both a brother and a father, and how awful he must feel. I wanted to find him and talk to him, but could understand that he needed to be near his family.

At dinnertime, Jack and I lined up outside the dining saloon with the other men, waiting for the women to be served first. When we finally got inside I saw my mother sitting with Mrs. Fortune and Mrs. Hays and her daughter. I crouched down beside Mother and spoke with her briefly. She still seemed dazed. She said that she had rested but hadn't slept.

I decided to join the three Fortune sisters who were sitting at a nearby table. They were a very subdued group. I thanked them for taking in my mother. "I don't think she's given up hope that my father has survived," I added quietly.

"Yes," said Alice Fortune, "our mother keeps talking about what a strong swimmer Charles is, and how he would have taken care of Father." Her tone of voice made it clear that she had accepted the news that there were no more survivors. I had spotted Alice's admirer, William Sloper, on the deck of the *Carpathia,* but thought it better not to mention him. The fact that he had survived while her brother had not, would no doubt be painful for her.

The sisters soon finished their dinner and excused themselves, following my mother and theirs out of the dining saloon. I looked around the room for Jack and spotted Johnnie sitting with his sisters and Miss Bowen at a table near the wall. I stood up and waved to get his attention. When he looked up, I gestured to the empty seats at my table. He simply looked back down at his plate as if he had never seen me. I sat down, blushing.

"Best leave him be," said Jack, who had moved over to my table.

"I guess he's feeling very sad about his father," I replied.

"Oh that . . . and more," sighed Jack. "Some idiot asked him if he dressed like a girl to get off the *Titanic.*"

"No! I can't believe it," I said. "That's just awful." This made me more determined than ever to talk to Johnnie before we reached New York.

After dinner, Jack and I walked around the ship, wondering where we might stretch out for the night. The *Carpathia* passenger who had lent us her cabin earlier had now taken in a woman and her child. We looked into the lounge but saw that it was full of women. Some of them had pulled the cushions from the sofas to use as pillows.

"Maybe we should try the smoking room," said Jack. "That's usually a male domain."

The smell of stale cigar smoke hung in the air of the smoking room, but some men had already stretched out on the floor. Loud snoring noises were coming from a young fellow who was asleep on a pile of blankets.

"Do you gents have any spare blankets?" said a female voice behind me.

I turned to see three young women who had just entered the room. I pointed to the snoring fellow hogging the pile of blankets.

"Of all the cheek!" said one of them. She stalked over and yanked on the blanket just beneath him. He rolled onto the floor with a thump and began cursing loudly.

"And to think such as you were saved!" scolded the girl. We all applauded as the red-faced man made a hasty exit. Jack and I each took one blanket from the pile he had left, and I curled up under a table, using my sweater as a pillow. With my bruised back I had to sleep on one side, but I was soon fast asleep, though not for long. Someone decided to use the table above me as a bed. I woke up when I heard him wriggling about, trying to get comfortable. I dozed off again, but he kept getting up during the night and clomping off, only to come back and thump around again overhead. How can anyone need to pee so often? I wondered. I thought of moving, but sleeping bodies surrounded me. Too soon, morning light seeped through the smoking room's portholes.

"Did you sleep much?" asked Jack groggily as I joined him in the line for the toilet.

"Not much," I replied, yawning. "The fellow on the table above me kept thumping on and off it all night long."

"That's Norris Williams," he said, gesturing with his head as Williams clomped out of the room once again. "I heard that his legs are badly frostbitten. The ship's doctor wanted to amputate them, but Norris refused. He's determined to exercise them day and night."

"But — "

"He's a champion tennis player and wants to play Wimbledon."

I said nothing but felt my face redden. What was losing a little sleep compared to losing your legs?

We ran into Williams again that morning as he limped very deliberately around the deck. His family and Jack's knew each other, as they were from the same area outside Philadelphia. We talked about the sinking and Norris told us that just after he hit the water, he had come face to face with a British bulldog.

I thought of the beautiful bulldog I'd seen in the kennels. So someone did release the dogs. At least Max hadn't drowned in his cage.

Norris went on to describe how he had caught sight of what looked like a boat and had swum toward it. It turned out to be a collapsible half full of water. This must have been the other collapsible that had been lashed to the roof of the officer's quarters, I thought. Norris had had to cling to the side of it for a while before someone hauled him into it.

"We sat in freezing water over our knees for hours," he said. "When we were finally picked up by another lifeboat, there were only eleven of us still alive. About twenty others had died from the cold."

We were all silent for a moment. Then Jack and I described how several men had died from exposure and dropped off into the ocean from our overturned boat.

"Harold Bride was on your boat, too, wasn't he?" asked Norris. I nodded.

"He was in the infirmary with me yesterday," Norris continued. "His feet were frozen and bandaged. But someone came and said the *Carpathia*'s operator couldn't keep up with all the wireless messages, so Bride took a pair of crutches and hobbled off to help him. What a guy!"

"Do you think it's true that the *Titanic* received warning messages about icebergs ahead?" asked Jack.

"Bride never told me about that — " Norris began.

"It's true! They did!" I exclaimed. "I know they did! I went to the Marconi room on Sunday morning and I heard Bride say 'another ice message.' I had to ask my father what an ice message was."

"Makes you wonder why we were barrelling along at full speed on Sunday night then," Norris replied. "I think Mr. Ismay will have some explaining to do when we reach New York."

"I'd heard that Ismay got into one of the last lifeboats," said Jack, "but I've not seen him on board here."

"Nobody has. He's holed up in the doctor's cabin

and takes all his meals in there," said Norris, leaning over to massage his legs. "He's in complete shock, apparently. Losing his new ship has been too much for him."

The talk of wireless messages made me wonder if ours had gone through to Arthur in Montreal. They had given us Marconigram forms earlier, and I had taken one to breakfast and filled it out with my mother. *Jamie, Rosalie and I safe. No news yet of Father. Mother,* was the message she had agreed to send. I think my mother knew in her heart that she was a widow, but part of her still refused to accept it. She had also developed a bad cold and spent most of her time in the cabin she shared with Mrs. Fortune. Rosalie looked in on her frequently, but spent the rest of her time sewing blankets into clothes for the children who had escaped wearing only pyjamas or nightgowns. I had seen a few young children toddling about the ship wearing these makeshift robes.

"I 'ave heard people say the most cruel things," Rosalie confided to me. "They say of the third-class people, 'Why did they bother to save so many from steerage?' As if their lives were worthless!"

I shook my head sadly at this.

People were certainly talking more today, I noticed. And their stories about the sinking were already becoming exaggerated. I'd heard people say that the officers had been forced to shoot people to prevent them from rushing at the boats. Others claimed they were sure that Captain Smith had shot himself as the boat sank. And many people were convinced that the last tune the orchestra had played on the sloping deck was the hymn Nearer My God to Thee.

"I don't remember any hymns being played," said Norris.

"Neither do I," I replied. "Only dance music."

"It's not like we were all just standing on the deck, nobly waiting to die, while they played a hymn," added Jack. "I think most of us were trying to think of ways to survive. I know I was."

Later that afternoon, Jack and I carried blankets over our arms as we stood in a line, waiting to have a bath. We were planning to rinse out our smelly clothes in the tub and then wrap ourselves in blankets while they dried. Another *Carpathia* passenger had offered us the use of his cabin for a few hours.

"People seem as certain about the *Titanic* sinking in one piece as they do about the last hymn," Jack mentioned as we sat on a bunk in our blankets. "Yet we both *saw* her break apart."

"And *heard* it, too!" I added.

"And I sure wish I had a dime for every time I've

heard someone say that they had a strange feeling about the ship," Jack continued.

"I know! Can you believe it?" I replied, launching into an imitation of a woman I'd heard with a Cockney accent. "'Oi just *knew* there was somethin' wrong wiv' that ship the *moment* I set foot in 'er. Oi just *knew* it!'"

Jack laughed so hard he had to bury his head in a pillow. Every time he looked up, I'd say, "Oi just *knew* it!" and that would set him off again. I laughed too, realizing that I had barely even smiled in the last two days.

"We can hear you lads hooting all the way down the corridor," said the passenger whose cabin we were using, as he entered the room. Both Jack and I mumbled apologies. "Oh well," the man said. "It helps relieve the tension, I suppose."

"Sorry," I said, trying to keep a straight face. "We just can't believe all the crazy stories people are making up about what happened."

"I guess it's just human nature to exaggerate," replied the passenger. He introduced himself as Lewis Skidmore and told us that he was from Brooklyn, New York, where he was an art teacher. He and his wife were on their honeymoon.

"Some honeymoon!" said Jack.

Lewis replied that their European trip being

interrupted was a small thing compared to the tragedy we had just been through. He wanted to hear about our experiences on board the *Titanic*, so while our clothes dried we described what had happened to us.

"You're quite sure that she broke apart while sinking?" Lewis asked at one point.

"Yes, quite certain," replied Jack. "We've spoken to others who saw the same thing. Those who say it sank in one piece weren't as close as we were."

Lewis pulled out his sketchbook and began to make drawings as Jack and I gave him a step-by-step description of the sinking. He said he would work up these sketches and show them to us tomorrow. By the time we had finished, our clothes had mostly dried, so we thanked him for the use of his room, got dressed and headed for the line outside the dining saloon. I think the food supplies on board must have been getting a little stretched, since for Tuesday dinner there was only soup, some cold sliced meats and macaroni.

That night as Jack and I lay on the floor of the smoking room, we were awakened by a deafening clap of thunder. Norris fell off the table where he was sleeping. One or two others thought we had hit something and ran out on deck to make sure there hadn't been another collision with an iceberg.

The rain that followed the thunderstorm lasted all of Wednesday. A thick fog rolled in during the morning and the mournful honk of the ship's fog-horn only added to the glum mood on board. I tried walking on deck with Norris after breakfast, but the driving rain forced us back inside. The public rooms were very crowded and people were beginning to squabble with each other. Some of the women were now feeling very anxious about what awaited them after our arrival in New York. It was beginning to sink in that their husbands were gone and their lives were changed forever.

Around four on Wednesday afternoon I decided to get some fresh air out on the deck. I'd been feeling very cooped up in the smoking room even though I'd managed to borrow a good book to read. There weren't many people on deck due to the cold and the fog, but I immediately spotted Johnnie standing beside a lifeboat davit.

"Johnnie," I said, walking up behind him. "I'm so glad to see you!"

He turned, looking a little startled. "Oh, hullo," he replied very coolly.

"How are you doing?" I asked.

"I have to go," he said, trying to push past me.

"Stop, wait! *Talk* to me," I said, catching him by the arm as he tried to wriggle past me.

"I know you're feeling sad. I am too. But I thought we were friends."

"That was then," he replied. "Now you're a hero and I'm the boy who dressed like a girl to get off the *Titanic*."

"Oh, Johnnie, I'm no hero. I'm just lucky. And so are you," I said, holding him by the arm. "We have our lives, Johnnie! Just think how horrible it would be for your mother to have lost *two* sons *and* her husband." As he tried to get away from me I put both hands on his shoulders. "And you didn't dress like a girl — that's idiotic."

"I see. So now I'm an idiot as well as a coward," he snapped, pushing my hands away and brushing past me.

"Not *you*, Johnnie, the people who *say* such things are idiots," I called after him. "In a month or two, everybody will have forgotten about the *Titanic* anyway!"

But he was already well down the deck and headed for the door to the dining saloon. My heart was racing and my head pounding. Back in the smoking room, I spent almost an hour trying to calm myself down. Finally, I decided that I would write Johnnie a letter when I got home to Montreal.

He'll feel differently by then, I thought.

CHAPTER ELEVEN
ARRIVAL IN NEW YORK

Thursday, April 18, 1912, 8:30 a.m.

"We passed the Nantucket lightship early this morning," Major Peuchen announced at breakfast. "I'm told we shall be in New York harbour by this evening."

At his mention of New York I couldn't help but feel a tremor of excitement run up my spine. I'd always wanted to see New York! Although the *Carpathia* had felt like a safe cocoon since our rescue, I was tired of the hard floor in the crowded smoking room. And I was more than ready to get into some fresh clothes and sleep in a real bed once again. When I looked across the table at my mother, however, I saw a look of worry on her face.

"I'm sure we can find a hotel for tonight," I said, patting her shoulder.

She simply nodded and I realized that she was hoping against hope that my father would be waiting for us on the pier. I suddenly felt guilty for my excitement about New York. I also realized that it was now up to me to care for my mother. She had mostly recovered from her cold, but still seemed very frail — as if she had become an old woman since Sunday night.

"I'm planning to stay at the Waldorf," said the Major. "We can all go there in the same taxi, if you'd like."

"That's very kind," said my mother in a quiet voice.

The Waldorf-Astoria! I remembered Johnnie telling me that Mr. Astor was the owner of that famous hotel. It seemed strange that he would never see it again. I'd heard that his young widow, Madeleine Astor, was sharing the captain's cabin with Jack's mother. I thought back to how Mr. Astor's dog had spooked Sykes, leading to our mad scramble on the forecastle deck. Could that have been only a week ago? What kids we had been then, I thought to myself. Part of me felt that I could never be that carefree boy ever again.

As I stared at the scrambled eggs on my plate, it occurred to me that this would be our last breakfast on the *Carpathia*. And today, for a change, there was fruit, and ham and muffins on the menu. I guessed that the ship's galley had been scrimping earlier, for fear their supplies might run out.

I glanced around the room in search of Johnnie, but couldn't see him at any of the tables. I did spy a Pekingese dog that had survived, sitting with the American couple who owned him. There were two other lapdogs, I'd heard, that had also been carried into lifeboats.

"Imagine saving a *dog* when people were drowning!" was just one of the disapproving comments I'd overheard about this.

Some of the women who had lost their husbands seemed resentful of the men who had survived. "How did *you* get off the *Titanic?*" was a question I'd been asked more than once. No wonder Johnnie felt so defensive about it. Major Peuchen, too, had experienced this resentment, so much so that he had asked Officer Lightoller to write a letter for him, describing how he had ordered the Major into a lifeboat.

People were also talking about an English lord and lady named Duff Gordon, who, it was said, had escaped in "their own private lifeboat" with only three other passengers and seven crewmen in a boat that could have held forty. The survivors from this lifeboat had all posed for a photograph on the deck of the *Carpathia*. One of them had apparently called out "Smile!" as the photo was being snapped, which had drawn indignant remarks from people nearby.

The rain and fog continued all morning, so I retreated to the smoking room with my book. In the afternoon I took a walk on deck with Norris, whose legs seemed to be getting better each day. He talked about going to Harvard in the fall and getting back into shape so he could compete for the Davis Cup.

Our foghorn had been keeping up its mournful blasts all day and, at one point, I thought I heard another foghorn answering it from onshore. I listened quietly and then heard it again.

"That's probably coming from the Fire Island lighthouse," said Norris, "just off Long Island. I've been to the beach near there. We'll be home in a few hours, I think."

"Maybe *you* will," I replied. "We've got another day's travel to get home to Montreal. But I'll have to buy some new clothes in New York, first," I said, pulling on my salt-stained sweater.

"Yes," said Norris with a smile, "it's not like we have anything to pack up before we get off."

The *Carpathia* gave us one final supper and I sat once again with my mother and Major Peuchen. We were told that first-class passengers would be the first to disembark, and that the White Star Line would provide cars at the pier to take us to our destinations. We agreed to find Rosalie and then meet the Major on deck before disembarking together. My mother was wearing the same dress she had put on before leaving the *Titanic* on Sunday night. But she was luckier than many other women, who were still wearing nightgowns under their coats.

As we came closer to New York harbour in the early evening, a thunderstorm erupted, bringing down sheets of rain. I stood on an enclosed deck, hoping for my first look at the Statue of Liberty. But I only caught a few glimpses of it, illuminated by flashes of lightning. Other bursts of white light kept erupting from all the tugs and small boats that were crowding around us, from the magnesium flares that press photographers were using. The boats were also packed with reporters shouting at us through megaphones.

"Have you seen Mr. Ismay?" was one question that was yelled across the water.

"Is Mrs. Astor on board?" was another.

I looked at a few of the passengers standing by me near the railing and we all rolled our eyes. Clearly the *Titanic*'s sinking was bigger news than we had ever dreamed. Norris said that a reporter had even clambered onboard from the boat that had brought out the harbour pilot and that Captain Rostron was keeping an eye on him on the bridge. As the *Carpathia* passed by the southern tip of Manhattan, we peered through the darkness and saw thousands of people standing silently in the rain in Battery Park.

"Good heavens, what are all those people doing there?" someone asked.

"I think they're waiting for us," came the reply.

As we slowly approached the shore, the *Carpathia* went right past the pier marked Cunard Line and headed for another long terminal building that had White Star Line painted on it. We thought we were going to dock there, but instead we saw the *Titanic*'s lifeboats being lowered over the side. Four of them were loaded onto the deck of a tugboat and seven others were put in the water to be towed behind it. It seemed pathetic that these few boats were all that was left to deliver to the White Star Line. If only we had dodged that iceberg, I thought, horns would be blaring and all the fireboats would be shooting up geysers to salute the *Titanic*'s maiden arrival in New York.

Soon the engines started up again and slowly we moved back toward the Cunard pier for landing. The tugs gently brought the *Carpathia* in beside the dock and we heard the sounds of the two gangways being lowered. I met my mother and Rosalie by the forward gangway at just after nine p.m. and we looked around for Major Peuchen. He soon arrived with a woman who was carrying a baby. I didn't know who she was, but assumed that the Major must have offered to help her ashore.

The scene on the dock was almost unbelievable. Wooden barriers had been set up beside the gangways, creating two paths through the crowd into the Cunard terminal. Mother took one look at all the people waiting below and turned away. I gave her my hand and she clasped it tightly. The first passengers began to walk down the gangway, some of them wearing dressing gowns or wrapped in blankets. We heard names being shouted out by the crowd and saw a few people being greeted with joyful hugs. At the top of the gangway, I turned and looked at the Major. He nodded back. Rosalie went first and I escorted my mother behind her. When we reached the dock we were surrounded by a sea of faces illuminated by white lights. Suddenly Arthur was standing in front of us.

"Arthur!" my mother called out. "Have you any news of Father?"

He simply lowered his eyes and shook his head. I heard my mother stifle a low cry and felt her crumple beside me. Arthur quickly grabbed her and put his arm around her waist. She rested her head on his shoulder for a minute and then walked beside him into the terminal. I looked behind me for Major Peuchen but saw that he was off to one side talking to reporters.

"Carelessness, gross carelessness!" I heard him say, and thought to myself that the reporters had found their man.

When I stepped inside the terminal, Arthur turned to me and asked for the landing cards we'd been given on the *Carpathia*. I pulled them out of my pocket and he quickly took them and gave them to the customs official. I told Arthur that we were going to the Waldorf-Astoria and that the White Star Line would cover our expenses.

"I have reserved rooms there for us already," he said briskly. From his manner it seemed clear that he saw himself as the man in charge. I looked at Rosalie and saw her raise her eyebrows in a sympathetic glance.

"It's a mob scene out there," said Arthur as we walked toward the front door of the terminal. He was right. When we stepped onto the street, we were almost blinded by the photographers' flares. Hundreds of policemen had linked arms to hold back a crowd that I later learned was more than thirty thousand people.

"Are you the boy that dressed as a girl?" a reporter yelled, shoving his face so close to me that I could smell his breath.

"I'll pay you for your story, son!" someone else called out.

Arthur turned and pulled me by the hand, although I was managing perfectly well on my own. We made our way to a taxi and all four of us got in, with Rosalie sitting up front beside the driver. The taxi driver kept honking his horn as we slowly made our way through the rainy, crowded streets.

"I don't understand," my mother said with a quaver in her voice. "Surely *all* these people can't have had relatives on the *Titanic?*"

"Oh, no, certainly not!" replied Arthur. "They're just curiosity seekers. The newspapers have been full of nothing but the *Titanic* all week. The unsinkable ship . . . all the million-aires who died — they can't seem to get enough of it."

"They're callin' it 'the story of the century,'" said the driver.

"How splendid that my husband's death is providing so much . . . entertainment . . . " my mother said before dissolving in tears.

"Oh, ma'am, I'm real sorry," the driver said. "I didn't know — "

"They've sent a ship out from Halifax to look for bodies," said Arthur, putting his arm around her. "I'm just praying we can bring him home for a proper burial."

Arthur was saying this to be comforting, but at the words "burial" and "bodies" my mother began to sob.

Oh, well done, Arthur, I thought. Only half an hour ago she was hoping to see Father standing on the pier.

Mother quickly forced herself to stop crying — embarrassed, I think, at making a scene in front of the driver. "So . . . there's no chance . . . at all . . . that he was rescued by another ship?" she asked.

"No, I'm afraid not," Arthur replied sadly.

"Poor . . . dear . . . Henry," was all she could say.

We sat in silence until we pulled up beside a huge red sandstone building with impressive arched doors.

"Welcome to the Waldorf-Astoria," said a uniformed doorman as he opened the taxi door next to me. "May I assist you with the luggage?"

"No luggage," I said with a shrug as he glanced at my grubby sweater.

"We've already registered," said Arthur.

The hotel's lobby was even grander than I'd imagined, with tall marble pillars, and an elaborate gilded ceiling. Arthur had reserved two suites, so we took my mother and Rosalie to theirs first and got them settled. Arthur's suite had a bedroom with a double bed, as well as a small room with a single bed designed for a maid or valet.

"I'll take the servant's room," I said to Arthur.

"There's no need — " he began.

"No, don't worry," I said. "It's a lot better than the floor I've been sleeping on."

The thought of a hot bath was very inviting, but I suddenly felt overwhelmingly tired. I stripped off my clothes, dived between the fresh sheets and fell into a deep sleep.

* * *

I ran myself a hot, soapy bath the next morning and was revelling in a good soak when Arthur walked in.

"We'll have to get you some new clothes," he said. "I can lend you a shirt and a jacket for the dining room this morning."

His clothes were a little big on me so I felt slightly odd as we went down to breakfast in the elevator. Arthur told me that my mother and Rosalie were having breakfast in their room. I noticed the black mourning band he was wearing around his arm and I thought I should probably get one too.

The lobby of the hotel was so full of people we had to wait for a table in the dining room.

"Very busy this morning, sir," said the waiter when we were finally seated. "We have senators here from Washington. They're holding an inquiry into the *Titanic* disaster in the East Room."

"Yes. I lost my father on the *Titanic*," replied Arthur.

I stared at him. I couldn't believe he'd said *my* father, not *our* father.

"Very sorry to hear that, sir," replied the waiter.

After breakfast, Arthur suggested we walk over to Macy's to buy me some new clothes. "It's only a few blocks away," he said.

In the hotel lobby a group of reporters surrounded Major Peuchen. His wife and son and daughter were with him. He was wearing a new set of clothes, which his family must have brought down from Toronto for him. "I have never uttered an unkind word about Captain Smith," I heard the Major saying. Then someone called my name. It was the Major, waving me over. I reluctantly turned toward him.

"This young man stood all night on an overturned boat," the Major said, pointing toward me.

I blushed as the reporters began firing questions at me. Arthur was standing back so I gestured to him for help. He quickly put his arm around my shoulders and we moved away from the huddle of reporters, but at the hotel doorway we had to fight our way through another pack of press people. "We're waiting for Ismay," I heard one of them say. "He's on the hot seat this morning!"

Arthur had told me at breakfast that J. Bruce Ismay was being savaged by the newspapers for having stepped into one of the last lifeboats.

"They need someone to blame," said Arthur, "and as the president of the White Star Line, I suppose he's it."

I'd replied that we hadn't seen Ismay at all on the *Carpathia,* and rumour had it that he was a nervous wreck.

As we walked along 34th Street, Arthur remarked, "Major Peuchen seems a fine man. I'm sure he was helpful to you and Mother."

"Yes, I suppose," I replied. "He should learn not to talk so much, though."

"And you, Jamie, should learn to be more respectful," Arthur said.

"And *you* shouldn't talk to me like I'm a child," I shot back.

We walked in silence until we reached Macy's. It was the biggest store I'd ever seen, and seemed to cover a whole city block. The front windows were draped in black bunting. Inside one was a framed photograph of an elderly couple with a sign that read, *Isidor and Ida Straus. Their lives were Beautiful and their deaths Glorious. Sadly mourned by all their employees.*

"Straus was an owner of Macy's," said Arthur. "They both died on the *Titanic*."

"I know," I said, suddenly remembering the elderly woman who had stepped out of the lifeboat to stay with her husband. "I saw them together at the end."

But Arthur just looked at me skeptically, as if I was making it up.

* * *

I had never been much of a newspaper reader, but over the next two days I devoured every paper I could get my hands on. The *Titanic* story seemed to fill most of their pages and I couldn't believe how much of the information was completely false. The papers said that William Sloper had dressed in women's clothes to get into a lifeboat, which I knew was untrue. J. Bruce Ismay was also taking a pounding for the evasive answers he'd given at the Senate Inquiry on Friday. One newspaper showed a photo of him surrounded by pictures of *Titanic* widows with the caption *J. BRUTE Ismay*.

For the train trip home to Montreal, Arthur had bought a stack of newspapers. I took them to a seat far away from Mother, since I knew they would upset her. We had stayed in New York until Sunday because she had spent most of Friday and Saturday in bed, exhausted and grieving. In one newspaper was a picture of the Marconi operator Harold Bride being carried off the *Carpathia* with bandaged feet. I read about his testimony before the Senate Inquiry on Saturday, describing the last hours in the Marconi room.

Every paper seemed to have a picture of two French toddlers who were dubbed "the *Titanic* orphans." I recognized them as the little boys that the man who called himself Mr. Hoffman had put into the last lifeboat.

When I turned to the Sunday newspapers, I found something that surprised me more than anything. Beside a photograph of Jack Thayer was a series of six drawings headlined *How the* Titanic *Went Down.* The information was credited to Jack Thayer and the drawings to Lewis Skidmore.

"Oh no!" I said, so loudly that people on the train turned to look at me. Had Jack even seen these? I wondered. If I had looked at them I would certainly have made some corrections. The first drawing showed the *Titanic* running up onto a giant mountain of ice. The third showed it breaking in two in the middle with the bow and stern both popping upwards. Although I've never been much of an artist, I immediately took out my pen and began correcting them. Maybe I could get a newspaper in Montreal to print more accurate versions of the drawings.

After a few more hours, the train slowed as we approached the Canadian border. There, we all had to get out and walk through a customs shed. When the customs agent saw the black arm bands Arthur and I were wearing, and my mother and Rosalie dressed in black, he waved us through with a sympathetic look.

Several hours later, I looked out the window and saw that we were arriving on the outskirts of Montreal. The city looked familiar as the train pulled into the station. And our house in West-mount seemed unchanged when the taxi pulled up in front of it.

But I knew that for me, nothing would ever be the same again.

CHAPTER TWELVE
A JOURNEY TO HALIFAX

May 1, 1912

"They've found Father's body," my mother said, with a tremble in her voice. "Arthur is going to Halifax to bring him home."

"I'm going, too," I replied.

"Oh, Jamie, no, it might be rather upsetting — " she began.

"Worse than surviving the *Titanic?*" I asked. "I don't think so."

"I'm not sure Arthur will want to take you — "

"I don't need to be *taken,* Mother. I'm not a child," I said.

Suddenly Arthur came thundering down the staircase from the top floor. "There's absolutely *no* need for *two* of us to go to Halifax!" he called out from over the banister. "I'm *perfectly* capable of handling it!"

"I'm sure you are — " my mother said.

"But you weren't *there,* Arthur," I insisted. "I was with him at the end," I added, my voice breaking a little, "and I want to bring him home."

There was a brief silence, broken only by the sound of my mother weeping softly into her handkerchief.

"Please, Arthur," she said through her tears. "Please . . . just . . . take him with you."

Arthur let out a long sigh and then stormed down the rest of the stairs and out the front door, slamming it behind him.

Mother went into the parlour and closed the sliding doors — she didn't like the servants to see her weeping.

When he came home after work that evening, Arthur stuck his head into my bedroom, where I was lying reading on the bed. "The train leaves at eight forty-five tomorrow morning," he announced coolly. "We'll spend a night on the train and a night in Halifax, so pack a bag."

He was still sulking at dinner, so it was a gloomy meal for just the two of us, since Mother was having a tray sent up to her room. My brother was taking his new role as head of the household just a little too seriously for my liking. And although I didn't dare say so, it seemed to me that he was almost enjoying the attention and sympathy he was receiving for having lost a father on the *Titanic*. The day after we returned from New York he had attended a memorial service for the Allisons, even though he barely knew them.

"I went to represent the family," he told me when I asked him about it. "Father knew Hudson Allison through the bank. He would have wished me to attend."

The Montreal newspapers had been full of stories about the Allisons, since Hudson Allison, a successful local businessman, had perished on the *Titanic* along with his wife and three-year-old daughter. Only their infant son Trevor had survived. When I saw a newspaper photo of a nursemaid holding Trevor, I immediately recognized her as the woman who had disembarked with a baby from the *Carpathia* beside Major Peuchen. One exaggerated headline claimed *With Orphaned Babe In Arms Major Arthur Peuchen Steps Ashore.*

Many of the newspapers ran a photograph of Hudson Allison with his wife, Bess, and daughter, Loraine. I remembered seeing this quiet young family sitting with Major Peuchen and Mr. Molson in the dining saloon on the last night. The newspapers were saying that the nursemaid had taken Trevor into a lifeboat without telling Mrs. Allison. She had reportedly searched frantically for her baby, and by the time she discovered that Trevor had already gone with his nurse, all the boats had left. As I stared at the Allison family photograph, I thought of little Loraine clinging to her mother as that giant wave washed up the slanting deck. It made me shudder.

Major Peuchen's name had been in the newspapers almost every day since our arrival in New York. *Major Peuchen Blames Captain Who Went Down With His Ship* was the headline to one article that quoted him saying that Captain Smith was guilty of "criminal carelessness." Then the next week, the Major had made headlines again after he told his story before the U.S. Senate Inquiry. At the end of his testimony he had read out a statement claiming that he had never said "any personal or unkind thing about Captain Smith." During his questioning, Major Peuchen had also claimed that he saw the *Titanic* sink in one piece, supporting what now seemed to be the "official" view.

Appearing just before Major Peuchen at the inquiry was Frederick Fleet, the lookout who had spotted the iceberg from the crow's nest. He testified that the binoculars for the lookouts had gone missing the day the ship left Southampton. With binoculars in the crow's nest, he said, they might have seen the iceberg "soon enough to get out of the way." I added the missing binoculars to my mental list of all the *Titanic* "if onlys." If only they had paid attention to the iceberg warnings and slowed down. If only there had been enough lifeboats for everyone on board. If only that ship whose lights we had seen on the horizon had come to the rescue.

It now seemed clear to me that this "mystery" vessel was most likely the *Californian*, the ship that had shown up beside the *Carpathia* on the morning we were rescued. Three days after Major Peuchen appeared at the inquiry, Captain Lord of the *Californian* had been summoned for some intense questioning by the American senators. He stated that on the night of April 14 he had seen the ice field ahead of him and had stopped his ship's engines at 10:21 p.m. He decided to wait there until dawn. Just before 11:00 p.m. the men on watch had seen the lights of a large steamer approaching. Later they had seen eight white distress rockets being fired. They had tried signalling the ship in the distance with a Morse lamp but had received no reply. To make matters worse, their Marconi operator had gone to bed and no one had thought to wake him up. If someone had, he would have heard the *Titanic*'s distress calls and the *Californian* could have come to the rescue. If only that had happened, I thought, I wouldn't be heading to Halifax to collect my father's body.

As we waited for our train to arrive early the next morning at Bonaventure Station, Arthur went over to a newsstand and bought every paper on sale. He returned with his arms full and gave half of the stack to me. I knew that he was reading everything he could about the *Titanic* disaster. Yet never once had he asked me about my experiences on the ship or my last hours with Father.

Arthur and I had never been very close, because he was so much older and had been away at boarding school most of the time I was growing up. Now that he considered himself "the head of the family" he didn't seem to know what to do with me. I wondered if he thought I was just a child and too young to understand what had happened. Did he resent the fact that I had survived and that Father had not? Did he blame me for Father's death? All kinds of conflicting thoughts ran through my mind.

After we boarded the train, Arthur and I sat on either side of the aisle, silently immersed in our newspapers. As the train went along beside the St. Lawrence River, I looked out at the trees with their new green leaves and thought of the train journey from London to Southampton. Could it only have been three weeks ago?

When the conductor came by to check our tickets, he glanced down at the headlines of the newspaper on my lap. "A very sad business, the *Titanic*," he commented. "Last week every Grand Trunk train came to a stop for five minutes in honour of Mr. Hays, our president."

"Yes, I met Mr. Hays — " I started to say, but Arthur cut me off.

"Our father knew Charles Hays well," he said. "But he, too, died on the *Titanic*."

"Very sorry, sir," the conductor said, glancing at Arthur's black arm band. "Very sorry for your loss."

"No need to tell *everyone* our business, Jamie," Arthur muttered from behind his newspaper after the conductor had left.

"It wasn't *me* who told him a*nything*," I snapped, picking up another newspaper and rustling it angrily in front of my face.

At lunch in the dining car, Arthur was still not being very friendly. He told me that he had arranged for Father's funeral service to be held next Friday at Christ Church Cathedral and that he would then be interred in the family plot in Mount Royal Cemetery.

After lunch I returned to my newspapers and read about J. Bruce Ismay's second appearance at the U.S. Inquiry on April 30. The senators had grilled Ismay as to whether he had encouraged Captain Smith to increase the *Titanic*'s speed.

Johnnie Ryerson's mother had been quoted in a newspaper as saying that Ismay had showed her an ice warning message and told her that they were speeding up to get through the ice field. Ismay denied saying this. Reading about Mrs. Ryerson made me think of Johnnie. I decided to write him a letter as soon as I got back home.

*　*　*

As our train pulled into Halifax early the next morning I felt surprisingly rested after my night in the sleeping car. When I had first climbed into my bunk I wasn't sure how well I'd sleep, but the rocking motion of the train had soon sent me to dreamland.

"We'll go to the hotel first and leave our bags there," Arthur announced as we stepped onto the platform. We checked into the Waverley Hotel on Barrington Street, then took a taxi to the Mayflower Curling Rink on Agricola Street, which had been converted into a temporary morgue. Like many buildings in the city, the rink was draped in black bunting. Outside it stood a line of horse-drawn hearses.

"Sorry, sir, very busy today. We're having our first interment at Fairview Cemetery this afternoon," said the man who greeted us. He was sitting behind a desk in a room where spectators usually sat to view the curling matches. Arthur gave him our name and the man scanned through his list and whispered to an assistant, who soon came back with a brown envelope. Inside it was a gold wedding band, a pair of cufflinks and a pocket watch inscribed with the initials J.K.L.

"That's my father's watch," said Arthur. "It was my grandfather's originally. Those are his initials on it."

"Perhaps that is why there was some confusion regarding identification," said the man at the desk. Another person soon came and led us to an upstairs office where there were forms to be filled out. Eventually we were ushered onto the floor of the curling rink, which was divided by canvas partitions that each enclosed three coffins.

A strong medicinal smell filled the air. I realized this must be from the embalming fluid used to preserve the corpses. Inside one of the canvas cubicles, the wooden top to a plain pine coffin was lifted off. I gasped a little when I first saw my father's body. His eyes were closed and his face looked very calm, though very white. He was wearing the black overcoat that he had put on over his pyjamas in our stateroom. Dried salt still clung to the collar.

"Yes, that's him," I said quickly.

Arthur shot a look of irritation at me. "That is indeed our father," he confirmed in a dignified voice.

"I'd like to make arrangements for the remains to be transferred to Montreal."

"Very good, sir," replied the undertaker's assistant as the lid of the coffin was replaced.

We returned to our hotel in silence. There was an utter finality to the sight of our father's body that was very sobering.

That evening we had a quiet dinner in the hotel and then went to bed. Later that night I woke up because I heard a sound in our room. I sat up and looked around. A crack of light was coming from below the bathroom door. Then the noise came again and I realized it was the sound of sobbing. Through the bathroom door I could hear Arthur trying to stifle his grief, only to have it break out in a low wail, followed by several sharp intakes of breath. Eventually I heard him blow his nose, so I quickly fell back on my pillow as he returned to bed. I wondered if I should say something to try to comfort him. But I knew that he would only be embarrassed if he thought I had heard him weeping.

The next morning Arthur was already dressed and ready to go down to breakfast when I stepped out of bed in my pyjamas.

"Can I tell you something?" I asked, putting my hand on his shoulder as he stood by the door. Before he could answer, I continued. "I want to tell you about Father's last words to me on the *Titanic*. He said, 'Be sure to tell Arthur I love him.' He also told me not to worry, because, 'Arthur will take care of things.' That's what he said."

Arthur looked a little startled. His eyes began to fill with tears. He quickly turned his head away and left the room. I had exaggerated what Father had actually said, but I felt it was what he had *meant* to say.

Arthur never responded to what I told him, nor did I ever raise the subject with him again. But I felt a thaw in his attitude toward me on the trip home and during the days and weeks that followed. Our shared grief over Father's death could have brought us closer together as brothers — but it didn't. Talking about feelings and emotions wasn't something men did very easily in those days. That September I went off to Bishop's College School and Arthur was soon transferred to a bank in Toronto. He enlisted as an officer when World War I broke out in August of 1914. Exactly three years and one week after the sinking of the *Titanic,* he was killed in a poison gas attack near the town of Ypres in Belgium.

DISCOVERY
September 3, 1985

"I've brought you *all* the papers this morning, Dad," said my daughter.

"Yes, they've discovered the *Titanic*," I said calmly.

"You know?" she asked, somewhat disappointed.

"Heard about it on my clock radio this morning," I replied.

"Well, the first photos aren't all that thrilling," she said, dumping the newspapers in my lap. "They're kind of blue and fuzzy."

I stared down at a tabloid with the front-page headline *TITANIC* FOUND in red, and turned to a spread of colour photographs inside. One of them took my breath away. "Oh my goodness," I said, "will you look at that. Oh my, my, my . . . "

She looked over my shoulder. "What are you seeing? They don't look like much to me."

I pointed to one photograph. "*That.* That's the fo'c'sle deck up by the bow. Those are the anchor chains still stretched out on the deck from the two windlasses. Oh my. That's something I never thought I'd see again."

"But you didn't get up *there*, did you?" she asked.

"I was a boy, Marjorie," I replied. "Johnnie Ryerson and I got into all kinds of places on that ship."

"You've never told me about that," she said.

"Well . . . it was a terrible tragedy. Hundreds of people died, including your grandfather. So it didn't seem right to talk about it. And your grandmother would get very upset when people would even mention the name *Titanic*."

"What happened to Johnnie Ryerson?" she asked.

"I wrote him a letter after your grandfather's funeral," I said. "But he never replied. If he's still alive he'll be an old codger now, just like me."

"They say the wreck is lying in two pieces," said Marjorie. "So it's unlikely they'll ever be able to raise her."

"Just as well," I replied. "They should leave it alone. I saw her break in two, you know. So did Jack Thayer. But most people didn't believe us. I'm sorry Jack's not alive to see this."

"What happened to him?" Marjorie asked.

"Well, we kept in touch a little over the years. But he lost a son in the Pacific during the war and became very depressed. He took his own life in nineteen forty-five."

Tears sprang into Marjorie's eyes. She was no doubt thinking about her older brother Hank, who had also been killed in World War II. I had suffered greatly after that, as I'd been close to Hank in a way I never was with my own father. My wife never really recovered from it. I think it contributed to her early death over twenty years ago.

"You've experienced so much history, Dad," Marjorie said. "Someone should write it all down."

"Well, people *have* called up wanting to interview me about the *Titanic*," I replied. "It just never seemed right to talk about it, to me. But maybe now, I could . . . "

As if hearing my words, a reporter from the Montreal *Gazette* telephoned me only an hour or so later. He was writing a story about all the Montreal connections to the *Titanic* story and wondered if he could come by and talk to me. He sounded a pleasant fellow on the telephone, so I agreed to see him that afternoon. We spent an enjoyable few hours together and he even told me some things about the *Titanic* I hadn't known.

He asked me if I ever dreamed about the *Titanic*. I said that I had when I was younger, but not in recent years. Sometimes the roar of a crowd at a hockey game would remind me of the cries of all the people after the sinking. "It was the most unearthly sound I've ever heard," I said. "I can hear it still."

He told me that he just couldn't understand why more boats didn't go back to pick up people from the water. I had to agree. That was the one great question about the *Titanic* for which no one really had an answer.

As he was leaving, the reporter told me that he had interviewed one of Rosalie's daughters out in Outremont. Rosalie had left my mother's employment shortly after we returned home in 1912, and had married and had many children. When she died about ten years ago, I attended her funeral. One of her sons told me that the family had kept several different dogs when he was a boy, but that Rosalie always insisted they be Airedales. This had made me smile. I explained to him how fond Rosalie had been of our dog, Maxwell, who had died on the *Titanic*.

The reporter asked if I had any family photographs or memorabilia to accompany his article. I said that I would have to look through some of the trunks and boxes in the basement. "Living in the same house all your life means you accumulate a great deal of stuff," I told him.

Since my bad knees made it hard for me to get down the basement stairs, Marjorie came over with my granddaughter, Louise, and they brought up box after box of old family albums for me to look through. I heard squeals of pleasure from down below when Louise discovered some of my mother's huge old hats still trimmed with ostrich feathers.

I found a few treasures of my own. One of them was a 1912 photograph of me in my Winchester College uniform with that ugly straw hat. Another was the now-yellowed Marconigram sent from the *Titanic* to Arthur with the message: *Greetings from Titanic. In NY Wed. Arrive Montreal Thurs. Father.*

But the thing that pleased me most of all was a crumbling copy of an April 1912 newspaper with Lewis Skidmore's drawings of Jack Thayer's description of how the *Titanic* sank. In the margin, you could still see the rough pencil drawings I had made, correcting some of Skidmore's mistakes. I wasn't sure if this would interest the fellow from the *Gazette,* but he became quite excited about it.

"You're sure this is authentic?" he asked me.

I simply smiled. "Of course."

To my surprise, this old newspaper with my crude drawings made news all around the world. *Teenaged Boy Saw* Titanic *Break in Two But Was Not Believed Till Now* was an often repeated headline. It was a big scoop for the *Gazette* reporter, who sent me several envelopes of clippings after his story was picked up in places like Japan and Saudi

Arabia. CBC radio called and interviewed me for a program about the *Titanic*. Before long, I had to get Marjorie to install an answering machine for me, since my phone rang almost constantly with requests for interviews from journalists and TV shows. To my surprise, I discovered that there were even organizations for people interested in the *Titanic*. As the last Canadian survivor, I was invited to attend some of their memorial dinners and conventions. At my age, it's difficult for me to travel, but all the attention did provide an old man with some diversion.

Marjorie put all the newspaper and magazine clippings into a shiny new album and presented it to me proudly. As I looked through its pages I thought back to my last words to Johnnie Ryerson. "In a month or two, everybody will have forgotten about the *Titanic*, anyway!"

I couldn't have been more wrong. Hardly a day has passed in the last seventy-three years when I haven't thought about the *Titanic*. How could so many seemingly random occurrences have come together to cause such a tragedy? Why was I saved from that icy black water when over fifteen hundred others were not? I find myself unable to answer these questions. But every day they remind me of how fragile human life is — and how precious.

HISTORICAL NOTE

A century after its sinking, the *Titanic* continues to fascinate the world. Although most people know that the giant liner hit an iceberg and sank on its maiden voyage, far fewer are aware of how the ship came to be built in the first place.

The plan to build the world's largest liner was hatched during a dinner party at the London mansion of Lord William Pirrie in the summer of 1907. Pirrie was the chairman of Harland and Wolff shipbuilders, and his guest that evening was J. Bruce Ismay, the director of the White Star Line. Much on the two men's minds was a fast and elegant new ship called the *Lusitania* that was owned by White Star's chief competitor, the Cunard Line. After dinner, Pirrie and Ismay decided that they would build three new ships that would be larger and even more luxurious than the *Lusitania*. Within a year, Harland and Wolff had drawn up plans for two giant ships, and by mid-December of 1908, the keel plate for the first liner, the *Olympic,* was laid down. On March 31, 1909, the same was done for a sister ship, to be called the *Titanic*. A third, the *Gigantic*, was to be built later.

On the morning of May 31, 1911, a crowd of more than a thousand people gathered at the Belfast shipyards of Harland and Wolff for the launching of the *Titanic*. At five minutes past noon a rocket was fired just before the 23,600-tonne hull began to slide into the River Lagan to cheers and the blowing of tugboat whistles. Soon the *Titanic*'s hull gently rocked in the river while the newly completed *Olympic* waited nearby. That same day the *Olympic* left for Liverpool to prepare for her maiden voyage from Southampton on June 14, 1911. Although the two liners were built to be almost identical, the *Titanic*, when finished, would be slightly heavier than the *Olympic*, making it the world's biggest ship.

Following its launch, the *Titanic*'s hull was towed to the outfitting basin, where over the next ten months the upper decks and funnels were added and all her fittings and furnishings installed. After midnight on April 4, 1912, the new liner arrived in Southampton, where some final painting and finishing would be done in preparation for her maiden voyage on April 10.

As the *Titanic* moved alongside the pier shortly after noon on sailing day, it approached two smaller ships, the *Oceanic* and the *New York,* moored together at the dock. The passing of the huge new liner caused the *New York* to snap her mooring lines and swing out into the *Titanic's* path. Soon there was only about 1.2 metres separating them. A speedy order for full astern from the *Titanic's* bridge activated the portside propeller, causing a burst of water which allowed the giant ship to slide by safely. The tugboats then attached lines to tow the *New York* away. This near-collision delayed the *Titanic's* departure by an hour, causing her late arrival off Cherbourg that evening.

It was after dark when the *Titanic* departed from Cherbourg, having taken on 274 more passengers who had been brought out to the ship by tender. Among them were some of the *Titanic's* wealthiest travellers, including John Jacob Astor and his young wife, Madeleine; Arthur Ryerson and his family; and British aristocrats Sir Cosmo and Lady Duff Gordon. That evening as the lookouts went on duty in the crow's nest high up on the foremast, they noticed that the binoculars they had used for the Belfast to Southampton trip had gone missing. This was reported, but no one thought to replace them.

At approximately 11:30 the next morning, the *Titanic* arrived off Queenstown (today called

Cobh) in Ireland. Seven passengers disembarked there, including Francis M. Browne, an enthusiastic photographer and a candidate for the Jesuit priesthood. His photographs of the *Titanic* would become among the few surviving pictures actually taken on board the liner. Two tenders from Queenstown ferried out 120 passengers, most of them Irish immigrants travelling in third class, as well as 1385 sacks of mail. As the *Titanic* headed across the Atlantic, a young Irishman named Eugene Daly said goodbye to his native land by playing "Erin's Lament" on his bagpipes.

Over the next three days, the *Titanic* made excellent time through calm seas, and J. Bruce Ismay, who was on board for the maiden voyage, was very pleased with the new ship's performance. At 9:00 a.m. on Sunday, April 14, the *Titanic* received a radio warning of "bergs and field ice" ahead. Similar messages from other ships came in throughout the day. Apart from altering the ship's course to take a more southerly route, Captain Smith did not slow down or take any other special precautions. It was common practice at the time for ships to simply steer around icebergs when they were sighted.

At 11:39 that evening, lookout Frederick Fleet suddenly spotted a dark shape ahead. He rang the warning bell three times and telephoned the bridge to report, "Iceberg right ahead!" First Officer Murdoch quickly ordered the engines to be stopped and then reversed. The helmsman had already turned the ship's wheel sharply to avoid the approaching berg. Slowly, slowly, the ship began to turn. But then the officers felt a jolt and heard a grinding noise along the *Titanic*'s starboard side. Down in boiler room No. 6, icy water immediately shot through the punctured hull. The stokers there had to run for their lives as the watertight door to their boiler room began to close.

Captain Smith asked one of his officers to make an inspection tour of the ship. When he was told that the mailroom on G deck was flooding, he went to have a look for himself and there met Thomas Andrews, the ship's chief designer. Andrews knew that the *Titanic* was divided into sixteen watertight compartments and that it could float with any four of those breached. But he soon discovered that the first *five* compartments of the hull were filling with water. Since the walls between those compartments only went 3 metres above the waterline, Andrews knew the water would flow from one compartment into the next. He estimated that the *Titanic* had about an hour and a half left before she sank.

At about 12:27 p.m. Captain Smith asked the

senior radio operator, Jack Phillips, to send out a call for assistance. Three ships would respond to the distress call, the nearest being the *Carpathia*, which was 93 km away. Smith knew it would take the *Carpathia* hours to reach his ship. He also knew there were not nearly enough lifeboats for the more than 2200 people on board. Outdated regulations required the *Titanic* to carry only sixteen lifeboats. Even if all of these had been loaded to capacity, they would only have been able to carry approximately half of those on board. Most of the first lifeboats would leave the ship only partially filled, since "women and children only" was the order, and many women were reluctant to leave their husbands. They could also see the lights of another ship on the horizon that they thought would surely come to their rescue.

In addition to the sixteen regular lifeboats, there were four collapsible boats with canvas sides that could be raised. After the other lifeboats had left, two of these collapsible boats were placed in davits and left the ship heavily loaded at around 2:00 a.m. As the *Titanic*'s bow plunged under, passengers and crew struggled to free the two remaining collapsibles lashed to the roof of the officers' quarters. One floated off upside down, the other left awash but right side up.

By 2:20 a.m. the *Titanic's* stern was high in the air. Her lights blinked once and then went out forever. The ship then broke in two, between the third and fourth funnels. After the bow section disappeared, the severed stern fell back in the water before it, too, filled with water and sank. In the icy water over 1500 people floundered and cried out for rescue. But very few of the eighteen lifeboats came back to rescue swimmers. Twenty-eight men found refuge on the back of overturned Collapsible B and twelve survived after climbing into the half-submerged Collapsible A. When the *Carpathia* finally arrived just before dawn, it took aboard only 712 people from the 2209 who had been on board the *Titanic*.

As the *Carpathia* steamed toward New York, news of the *Titanic's* sinking made headlines around the world. The White Star Line chartered a small steamer, the *Mackay-Bennett*, to sail from Halifax on April 17 to search for bodies. It recovered 306 corpses, of which 116 were buried at sea because they were so badly decomposed. Three additional ships were sent out, but only twenty-two more bodies were found. Fifty-nine victims would eventually be claimed by relatives and sent home for burial, while the remaining 150 were interred in three Halifax cemeteries.

On the night of April 18, a crowd of over thirty thousand people mobbed the Cunard pier in New York to greet the arriving *Carpathia.* Waiting to meet J. Bruce Ismay were two American senators, with a summons for him to appear the next day before a U.S. Senate inquiry into the disaster. Ismay had stepped into one of the last lifeboats and would become a target of much criticism. The Senate inquiry lasted until May 25 and questioned eighty-two witnesses. It concluded that the ship whose lights had been seen from the *Titanic* was the *Californian,* and that it could have come to the rescue in time. It also recommended that ships should carry enough lifeboats for everyone on board, that regular lifeboat drills should be conducted and that the wireless equipment on ships should be in operation twenty-four hours a day.

Similar recommendations were made by a British inquiry that ran from May 2 to July 3 and questioned ninety-seven witnesses. The only passengers to testify were Lord and Lady Duff Gordon, who had been much criticized for escaping in a lifeboat that was less than one-third full. The British inquiry did not find fault with either the Duff Gordons or with Bruce Ismay, nor did it assign any blame to the White Star Line. It also found no evidence that third-class passengers had been treated unfairly, despite the fact that 536 of the 710 aboard were lost.

After the *Titanic* disaster, her sister ship *Olympic* was renovated to make her double hull truly watertight, and forty-eight additional lifeboats were added to her decks. The *Olympic* then had a long, successful career until 1935, when she was scrapped and her elegant furnishings were sold at auction. The third sister ship was completed in 1914 and named the *Britannic*, instead of the *Gigantic*. But she never carried any paying passengers. At the outbreak of World War I the *Britannic* was converted to a hospital ship and sunk by an enemy mine off Turkey on November 21, 1916. In August of 1995, Dr. Robert Ballard, the leader of the team that had discovered the *Titanic* ten years before, explored the wreck of the *Britannic* in a small nuclear submarine.

The *Titanic*'s wreck site has been visited many times since its discovery in 1985, and artifacts from it now appear in touring exhibitions. The last *Titanic* survivor, Millvina Dean, died in May 2009 at the age of ninety-seven.

GLOSSARY

A deck, B deck etc: The decks on the *Titanic* were numbered downward from A through G, with A deck being the first deck below the boat deck.

aft: toward the back or stern of a ship.

boat deck: the deck on a ship where the lifeboats are stored. On the *Titanic* this was the top deck.

boater: a stiff straw hat with a flat top and a ribbon.

bow: the front end of a ship.

bridge: a structure or area toward the front of a ship, from which it is navigated.

bunting: patriotic, festive or funeral decorations, usually made from cloth.

cabin: a room on a ship.

crow's nest: a lookout platform high on a ship's mast.

davits: crane-like arms used to raise and lower lifeboats.

forecastle: an area at the bow of a vessel; also called **fo'c'sle.**

forward: toward the front end of a ship.

funnel: a tall smokestack on a ship.

gangway: a ramp from a dock onto a ship.

gunwale: the upper edge of the side of a boat.

magnesium flares: an early form of flash photography.

Marconi room: a cabin on the boat deck where the two wireless (radio) operators worked.

militia: a volunteer military force.

Morse code: a system of dots and dashes representing letters and numbers, thus allowing messages to be transmitted by radio or flashing lamp.

port: the left side of a ship when facing the bow.

promenade: an upper deck that is sometimes enclosed, where passengers can walk.

starboard: the right-hand side of a ship when facing forward.

stern: the rear end of a ship.

tender: an auxiliary ship that ferries passengers or provisions to a larger ship.

well deck: a space on the deck of a ship lying at a lower level; on the *Titanic* there was one below the forecastle deck near the bow and below the rear deck at the stern.

windlass: a cylindrical device used for raising or hauling objects, around which a cable, rope or chain winds.

wireless: an early name for radio.

Two Winchester College boys in their straw hats that were called "strats."

Millionaire John Jacob Astor takes a walk with his young wife Madeleine and their Airedale terrier, Kitty.

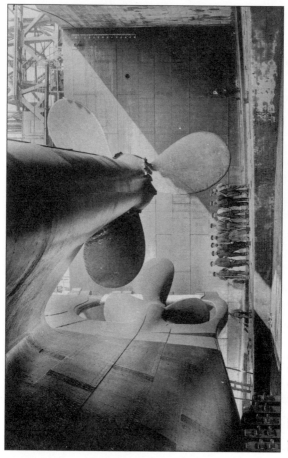

The Titanic had three giant bronze propellers. Each of the two side propellers was 7 metres across and weighed 34 tonnes. The centre propeller was slightly smaller.

The Titanic leaves Belfast for her sea trials on April 2, 1912. The testing of the new ship took only six hours. That evening, she left for Southampton to prepare for her maiden voyage.

Jack Thayer (upper) and twenty-seven others huddled on an overturned lifeboat (opposite) until they were rescued. Charles Fortune (lower) died in the icy water; his body was never recovered.

The crew of a ship that was sent from Halifax to search for bodies tried to recover the overturned lifeboat, but eventually set it adrift.

One of the Titanic's victims is prepared for burial. Of the 328 bodies recovered, 119 were buried at sea.

NO. 124   MALE   ESTIMATED AGE 50   LIGHT HAIR & MOUSTACHE.

CLOTHING Blue serge suit; blue handkerchief with "A.V.";
belt with gold buckle; brown boots with red rubber soles;
brown flannel shirt; "J.J.A." on back of collar.

EFFECTS Gold watch; cuff links, gold with diamond;
diamond ring with three stones; £225 in English notes;
$2440 in notes; £5 in gold; 7s. in silver; 5 ten franc
pieces; gold pencil; pocketbook.

FIRST CLASS.   NAME J.J. ASTOR

Sex- Male   Estimated age 60. Hair grey, bald.
Clothing- blue overcoat, and blue suit, white dress waistcoat,
black boots and purple socks. Two vests marked "R.A." and pink
drawers also marked "R.A."
Effects- Watch, chain and medals with name on;keys, comb, knife,
eyeglass case. 27:0:0 in gold, $20 gold piece and $64 in notes
1st Class.

                          Name,Ramon Artagaveytia
                          Alfredo Hetzfreey

*The bodies were given numbers in the order that they were
found; their personal effects were saved and listed. John
Jacob Astor was Number 124. Ramon Artagaveytia, a
businessman from Uruguay, was Number 22.*

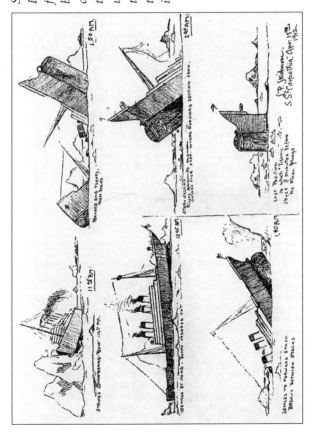

Sketches drawn by Lewis Skidmore from a description by Jack Thayer correctly show that the Titanic broke up while sinking, though many of the details are inaccurate.

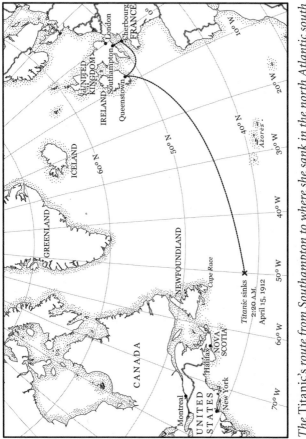

The Titanic's route from Southampton to where she sank in the north Atlantic south of Newfoundland.

IMAGE CREDITS

Grateful acknowledgment is made for permission to reprint the following.

Cover cameo: (detail) *Sons of George Cartwright, Calgary, Alberta,* Glenbow Archives, NA-1447-29.
Cover background (detail): Mono Print © 1999 topham Picturepoint.

Page 180: Winchester boys in boaters, courtesy of John Loewen.
Page 181: *Madeleine and John Jacob Astor,* Brown Brothers, PIX 676.
Page 182: *Port propeller and centre propeller of* Olympic *with posed workers and caisson from dock floor, April 1911,* © National Museums Northern Ireland 2011, Collection Harland & Wolff, Ulster Folk & Transport Museum HOYFM.HW.H.1512.
Page 183: *Titanic,* Brown Brothers, PIX 428.
Page 184 (upper, detail): *Jack Thayer with 1915 rowing team,* University of Pennsylvania Archives, 20050914019.
Page 184 (lower, detail): *Charles Fortune,* courtesy of Bishop's College School Archives.
Page 185: © The Titanic Historical Society.
Page 186: *Body of R.M.S.* Titanic *victim aboard rescue vessel* Minia *being made ready for make-shift coffin, 1912;* Reference no.: NSARM Photograph Collection: Transportation & Communication: Ships & Shipping: R.M.S. *Titanic* #2.
Page 187 (lower): *Description, clothing and effects of Body No. 22, first class passenger Ramon Artagaveytia;* Medical Examiner, City of Halifax and Town of Dartmouth NSARM RG 41, Vol. 75, no. 22.
Page 188: Sketches by Lewis Skidmore.
Page 189: Map by Paul Heersink/Paperglyphs.

The publisher wishes to thank Barbara Hehner for checking additional factual details.

Author's Note

In this novel, Jamie Laidlaw, his family and Rosalie are fictional characters. All the other people who appear in the story are real and I've attempted to describe them and their experiences as accurately as possible. John Ryerson, for example, was indeed travelling home on the *Titanic* with his family because of the death of his older brother in a motoring accident. His adventures on the ship with Jamie and the pet rat, however, are the products of my imagination. For many years after the disaster, John Ryerson refused to speak about the *Titanic*. He died in January 1986.

Jack Thayer wrote a letter to Milton Long's parents describing the last evening he spent with their son on the *Titanic*. I have used his recollections and added Jamie Laidlaw to their company. Arthur Peuchen's experiences are also recreated from how he described them. Until his death in 1929, Peuchen had to endure accusations of cowardice for having lived when so many had died.

Francis M. Browne was ordained as a Catholic priest in 1915. He served as a chaplain during World War I and was awarded a medal for valour. Browne remained a keen photographer and, after his death in 1960, albums containing over forty-two thousand of his photographs were discovered. His *Titanic* companion, Jack Dudley Odell, lived until 1995.

The official opening of the Château Laurier Hotel in Ottawa was postponed due to the death of Charles Hays. Sculptor Pierre Chevré's bust of Wilfrid Laurier was installed in the lobby, though Chevré himself would die less than two years later, having never recovered from the shock of the sinking. By contrast, R. Norris Williams recuperated well and soon won several national singles and doubles tennis championships. He died in 1968.

Ethel Fortune, the eldest of the three Fortune sisters, was haunted for years by a vision of her brother Charles flailing in the icy water.

The two French toddlers who were dubbed "the *Titanic* orphans" were reunited with their mother after she saw a photograph of them in a newspaper. Their father, whose real name was Michel Navratil, had been taking them to America without her knowledge.

Captain Arthur Rostron was awarded several medals for his heroism on the *Carpathia* and later became the commodore of the entire Cunard Line. Charles Lightoller was never made a captain of any White Star ship. He did become a navy commander in World War I, and during World War II used his own yacht to rescue soldiers from the beaches of Dunkirk. He died in 1952.

* * *

I've been lucky enough to write and edit a number of books about the *Titanic*. In 1986 I worked with explorer Dr. Robert Ballard on his bestselling book, *The Discovery of the Titanic*. Part of my job was helping to identify the artifacts Dr. Ballard had seen on the ocean floor.

In 1988 I also helped to create Robert Ballard's first book for young readers, *Exploring the Titanic*. In working on both those books I met a remarkable *Titanic* artist named Ken Marschall and with him and *Titanic* historian Don Lynch, compiled a lavish volume entitled *Titanic: An Illustrated History*. This book helped inspire James Cameron to make his epic movie, *Titanic*. In 1993 I oversaw the creation of the popular children's picture book, *Polar the Titanic Bear*; a few years later I wrote two books about the lost liner: *Inside the Titanic* and *882½ Amazing Answers to All Your Questions About the Titanic*.

ACKNOWLEDGMENTS

I would like to acknowledge the debt I owe to my *Titanic* mentors: Robert Ballard, Walter Lord, Ken Marschall and Don Lynch. In addition to consulting all the books I worked on with these people, I also found excellent information in Alan Hustak's *Titanic: The Canadian Story.* The ever-useful website *Encyclopedia Titanica* was also a very handy online reference tool. John and Charles Loewen provided excellent information from their days at Winchester College, as did Suzanne Foster, the college's archivist. Thanks also to Merrylou Smith at Bishop's College school. And special thanks go to *Titanic* author and historian George Behe for his expert read of the text, and to my long-time colleague and editor, Sandra Bogart Johnston.

ABOUT THE AUTHOR

Hugh Brewster is the award-winning author of twelve books for young readers, including *Prisoner of Dieppe* in the I Am Canada series. It was named a Best Book for 2010 by *Quill & Quire* and *The Globe and Mail,* and was nominated for the Ruth and Sylvia Schwartz Award. His other awards include the Children's Literature Round-tables of Canada Information Book Award for *On Juno Beach* and an Honour Book designation for *Dieppe: Canada's Darkest Day of WWII;* the Norma Fleck Award for *At Vimy Ridge;* a Governor General's Award nomination for *Carnation, Lily, Lily, Rose;* a Silver Birch Award nomination for *Dieppe;* and Silver Birch and Red Cedar Awards for *Anastasia's Album.*

Other books in the
I AM CANADA Series

For more information please see the I AM CANADA
website: www.scholastic.ca/iamcanada